CW00429419

The Happy Little World Of Gays

Cool Erotica

Table of Contents

The Happy Little World Of Gays

Chapter 1 Nick Taylor

The reason why I chose to write about Nick Taylor as the first sex partner is because the encounter with him can only be described in one word: passion.

I met Nick Taylor in a bathhouse in City A. Speaking of this bathhouse, I have to mention the difficulties I went through to find this place that night.

I was on a business trip in City A, and a net friend sent me a message saying he happened to be in City A too and suggested meeting up and having some fun. However, at that time, I didn't seem to have much interest in him, but I wanted to have a passionate night with him, so I replied to his message saying, "I want to check out the famous bathhouse in City A." I said "check out," but deep down, I wanted to seek excitement.

He quickly replied, saying he wouldn't go, as he had been to the bathhouse the night before, and since it was Saturday, the bathhouse had performances that night, and he had been fucked there multiple times that night, so he couldn't handle it again today.

Hearing him say that, I thought to myself: great, there must be some action there. So I asked him for the address of the bathhouse, and he told me the address, and specifically told me how to get there.

It was already 9 o'clock when I checked the time, so I thought there should be some good encounters at this time. So I followed the directions he gave me and started looking, but damn it, it was so difficult to find! It was already 11 o'clock at night, and I still couldn't find it. I thought, forget it, I'll just go back to the hotel and sleep.

Suddenly, at an intersection, three people appeared; one was young, and the other two were middle-aged. I took a closer look at the young one, who was wearing a particularly tight pair of jeans. From his appearance, I knew he was one of us and probably heading there too. So I followed behind the three of them and finally found the bathhouse.

The bathhouse looked small from the outside, and I didn't know if there would be anything interesting inside, but since I was already here, I decided to go in.

After entering, I changed my shoes, took a key, and walked inside. Then there was a staircase leading downstairs, and next to the staircase were lockers, where a few men were changing clothes. They had that unmistakably gay look and were staring at me. I think it was because it was my first time there, and they were probably hunting for fresh prey.

At this point, I should introduce myself to everyone so that you can understand why I became their target.

My name is Hunter. Actually, this is not my real name, just my online pseudonym. In City H, many people might recognize this username.

I am 27 years old, in that awkward stage between not young and not middle-aged, which is quite embarrassing. I am 190 centimeters tall, thanks to regular workouts at the gym during the past two years. In terms of physique, I would say I have a very standard one – well-defined where it should be and toned where it should be. I am quite satisfied with my own body. As for my looks... honestly, I'm not handsome.

Now, you might wonder why someone who isn't handsome can still get involved with so many gays. This probably comes down to my physique. In the bathhouse, everyone is directly exposed, and a simple glance can reveal length, girth, and thickness. I believe this is one of the best features of a bathhouse.

I took off my clothes and descended to the bottom of the stairs, heading straight to the shower area. The shower area had a rather futuristic design, with several short walls intersecting each other, providing the advantage of observing people from multiple angles.

There weren't many people showering, and none of them caught my attention. Just a few individuals with different body shapes in their thirties were showering, probably regulars here, occasionally exchanging jokes.

Beyond the shower area was a small sauna room. I walked in and found a couple of friends sitting inside. One of them had a towel covering his crotch, while the other was touching and exploring beneath his towel. Wow, they were pretty timid, not openly touching each other. I mean, who doesn't know what's going on?

They noticed my arrival, and the guy withdrew his hand, probably thinking I interrupted their fun. Then, another person in his thirties walked in and sat next to me, saying, "Is it your first time here, buddy?"

"Yeah," I replied. "Why are there so few people?"

"It's because of Sunday. Saturday is the busiest, with performances too."

"Oh, looks like I came for nothing today." I felt so frustrated at that moment.

"Why would you say that?" he said. "There are still some people upstairs."

"Upstairs?"

"Yes, upstairs is the resting area. It's dark up there, but there are still people. How about we go up and sit for a while?" He invited me.

But I wasn't interested in him, so I said, "You go up, I'll come later."

Seeing that I didn't follow him, probably thinking there was no chance, he left.

And the two men next me were getting more daring at this point. One of them came over and touched my cock. My cock was big, thick and very straight. I personally think it feels great, but several bottoms who have played with me say it's not satisfying enough. I guess it's because they've had lots of experiences. This man was touching my cock while also gripping another man's cock.

I said, "I don't like using hands, I prefer you to use your mouth to suck."

Perhaps he thought I was too direct because he hesitated and looked surprised.

I said, "What, don't you like sucking?"

Before I could finish my sentence, he leaned towards my crotch. His warm and soft lips enveloped my cock, and I pushed my cock a little harder into his mouth, instantly feeling the warm oral cavity stimulating my glans.

So warm, he wrapped his mouth around my cock, not too tight or loose, the pressure just right. My cock made a sound of friction sound.

He was really good at oral sex, igniting a burning desire within me, making me want to fuck his ass. But since there was another man next to us, I didn't say it directly.

Hearing my pleasurable moans, he started moving his mouth faster and faster, making me want to cum. But I thought to myself: I can't cum so easily right after coming in; I need to see if there are any other bottoms that I can fuck.

I couldn't hold back any longer. I pushed his head away, and he asked me in surprise, "Why didn't you cum?"

"I don't want to yet. The night is still young!" I replied.

His friend, upon hearing my response, laughed and said, "It's really your first time here!"

He turned to his friend and started servicing him with his mouth. His friend had a big cock, around 18 centimeters long. Looking at that tender and large cock, I was tempted to take it in my mouth. But alas, I couldn't accept it. I'm not used to sucking off others unless it's a man I really like.

Seeing them getting into it, I didn't want to bother them anymore. So I left the sauna room, rinsed my body, dried myself, and put on my clothes. Then, I headed upstairs.

After going up a narrow staircase, I arrived upstairs. The first thing I saw was a red curtain with lights outside. I entered the curtain, and it was pitch black inside. Rows of resting beds were arranged, with two small beds on each side and four small beds placed side by side in the middle.

Upon entering, I noticed a group of men gathered around the third bed in the middle row. As I approached, I discovered that three men were having sex on the bed. One chubby man was sticking his butt out, and another man was half kneeling, thrusting in and out of his body. The chubby guy also had another man's cock in his mouth.

It was too dark to see their faces clearly, but I could hear the wet sounds. It seemed like the chubby guy's ass was producing a lot of fluid, and you could tell by the sound the frequency of the thrusts. The chubby guy occasionally moaned.

Seeing them enjoying themselves, other men around them would occasionally touch the chubby guy's ass and feel the movements of the other man thrusting in and out. It felt terrifying here, where gays play crazily. It made me feel excited and passionate. It was uncomfortable not to do something. But despite the discomfort, I endured it and looked around to see if there was someone I liked. After circling the rest area, I discovered that there weren't many men, only nine or ten.

Damn it, I came at the wrong time. Why are there so few people? While thinking about what to do, I noticed someone with a decent physique, but because there was no light in the hall, I couldn't see his face, which was disappointing. After circling around and finding it uninteresting, I lay down next to the bed where the three men were having sex.

As I lay down, I heard someone shout, "I can't hold it anymore, I'm cumming."

Then came loud moans that kept getting louder, confirming that they were experiencing intense pleasure.

Hearing those sounds, I felt the air in the room permeated with the scent of semen, and everywhere, there were lascivious molecules. I thought it must be making everyone in the room boil with excitement.

After the three of them finished their encounter, two of them went downstairs, probably to clean up.

The crowd gradually dispersed, each going their separate ways to find their desired partners.

At this moment, the hall became quiet, and many people rested.

"Oh, looks like there's no chance, might as well sleep," I thought to myself.

Just as I was about to go to sleep, I suddenly heard footsteps approaching. I opened my eyes and saw the person with a decent physique that I had seen earlier. Could it be that he was coming towards me?

He had already arrived at the side of my bed and reached out to touch my chest, intentionally grabbing it. Since there was no one else I was interested in, I allowed him to continue even though I didn't know what he looked like. He touched my hand, and then his other hand began to roam under my armpit. I involuntarily closed my eyes, and I could feel myself getting excited. Then his hand moved down my abdomen, all the way to my cock. My body trembled uncontrollably as he slowly touched my cock.

He smiled and said to me, "Hey handsome, you're already aroused."

"It's because you touched me."

He squeezed me and said, "I'll make you feel good later."

"How will you make me feel good? Do it now."

As soon as I finished speaking, he lightly took my glans in his mouth and used his tongue to Circle Bround it. Instead of tightly enveloping my cock and moving up and down, he kept his mouth loose and completely enveloped the base, then tightly enveloped and released as he moved towards my glans. He repeated this pattern, exciting me and causing me to involuntarily make gasping sounds. It was the first time someone pleasured me in this way, and it felt amazing.

He was very skilled. Sometimes he used his tongue to lick my glans, sometimes he sucked on the tip, and sometimes he would take my testicles into his mouth. Other times he would lick the inner side of my thighs. He kept pleasuring me like this, causing my muscles to feel tense and on the brink of exploding.

Seeing that I was enjoying it, he asked, "Do you want to fuck my ass?"

"Do you have a condom? I didn't bring one since it's my first time here."

"I don't have one either."

"In that case, let's not do it without a condom."

"Oh."

He didn't say anything and continued to use his mouth to explore my genital area. He worked even harder, and in no time, I was on the edge of orgasm.

I lifted his head and said, "I'm about to come."

"Oh."

Then I asked him, "Can I come in your mouth?"

He said, "Okay."

With his consent, I forcefully pushed his head down. At that moment, I completely released myself, and streams of semen shot into his mouth. Even then, he seemed reluctant to leave my cock and continued to lick my glans.

"No, it's too ticklish."

I managed to free myself from his mouth, and he seemed to smile at me. Then he stood up and walked out of the hall.

It wasn't until this moment that I recovered from the pleasure of release. I realized that I never touched his body or his cock. To be honest, coming to the bathhouse for the first time, I felt that this place was too wild. There might be germs everywhere, and I was afraid in my mind.

I feel conflicted. Before ejaculation, I seem to lose my rationality, but once the milky semen sprays out, I suddenly feel empty and conflicted.

At this moment, the hall was strangely quiet, and I was tired as well. After rinsing my body, I fell into a deep sleep. I slept until morning and hastily went to shower before heading straight to the meeting place.

Like this, my night in City A came to an end. It was a wild night, my first time discovering this bathhouse in City A, and my first experience of the acceptance in a big city.

Nick Taylor was someone I met at the bathhouse for the second time, and it was a memorable and passionate encounter.

On that day, I was on a business trip in City A. After finishing my work, while shopping nearby, a City A online friend named Monroe sent me a message asking where I was. I told him my location, and around 3 o'clock, we met at the bookstore building. He was handsome and fair-skinned. He told me he was from City F and studying in City A. However, I wasn't interested in Monroe's type.

After chatting for a while, we wandered around mall, even though there wasn't much to see. Then we headed straight to the bathhouse.

When we arrived near the bathhouse, it was still early, so we had dinner at a nearby KFC. After hanging out for a while, it was around 6 o'clock according to the time, so we headed towards the bathhouse. We were worried about going too early and finding no one, which would be boring.

At the same intersection, we saw a boy who gave off a cool vibe. We said to each other, "He must also be going there."

As expected, we found out that he was familiar with the staff there and shouted at the entrance, "Guess what? I had a great time as Top last night! It became news!"

Monroe smiled and said to me, "He's wild."

We exchanged a smile.

We entered the bathhouse, and as we were changing our shoes at the front desk, a man was about to come down the stairs from upstairs. He glanced at the two of us. At first glance, he looked decent. His age was around 26 or 27, not very tall, about 170 centimeters, with fair skin, thick eyebrows, and large eyes.

I thought to myself, "Not bad." I didn't expect to meet him as soon as we entered - Nick Taylor.

Monroe and I walked in with our clothes and changed into the attire provided by the bathhouse in front of the lockers. We headed straight towards the shower area.

Since I wasn't interested in Monroe, we each found our own targets.

While I was showering, I suddenly saw him again: Nick Taylor. He was showering right next to me, chatting with two people around him. One of them was slightly chubby, around 29 years old (let's call him Chubby), and the other was attractive but also seemed older, around 30.

They seemed to be having a great time, and Chubby occasionally even jokingly touched Nick Taylor's cock. Nick Taylor's cock appeared to be around 9 or 10 centimeters in its flaccid state, and it seemed like it would be much larger when erect. I imagined it would feel great to touch, otherwise why would Chubby keep touching it? Nick Taylor was mischievous too, deliberately moaning, "Oh, oh," suggesting that it felt amazing.

I couldn't help but think, how could I start a conversation with Nick Taylor? I really wanted to go up to him and talk, and of course, touch his cock too.

After rinsing off, I approached the sauna, which was very narrow and had an extremely lascivious red light. Three people were already sitting on one side, and there was no space left. I had to sit alone on the other side. Once I settled down, I noticed that Nick Taylor and Chubby had also entered, but since there was no space, they kept standing. Chubby was really bold. Whenever he saw someone with a large member nearby, he would go over and touch their cock, saying, "Hey handsome, it's so big, so fun!"

At that moment, I sensed that Nick Taylor was deliberately moving closer to me and stopped very close to where I was. Maybe it was because of a nail on the wall that accidentally pricked him. He turned his head and said, "Ouch, that hurt!"

He picked up the wooden ladle used for water in the sauna and began pricking it into the wall. At that moment, his buttocks were facing me, so I cautiously used my fingers to lightly touch his body.

After Nick Taylor finished fixing the nail, he leaned against it. I dared not make any sudden movements, so I lightly touched his side with my fingers. Perhaps he felt my touch because he held onto my finger. I did it unconsciously, just extending one finger, and he grasped it tightly. Later, I wondered if this gesture made him understand that I was a top.

Once he held my hand, he became bold and started stroking my cock along the inside of my thigh.

Through the dense hair, he finally found my erect cock. He gently held it and started stroking it up and down. I couldn't help but lean my head against the wall. His touch felt amazing. At that moment, I tapped his head with my hand, signaling him to use his mouth. He pressed himself against my body and whispered in my ear, "Shall we do it here?"

I replied, "Yes, it's more exciting this way."

He glanced back at the others. Chubby was still pleasuring the handsome guy's cock, who occasionally let out sounds. The other two were also pleasuring each other.

After Nick Taylor saw this scene, I think he felt encouraged. He let go and crouched down, using his thick lips to wrap around my cock. As he took it in deep with each mouthful, my glans reached his throat. A warm flow began to surge in my abdomen.

Most people don't like deepthroating, but Nick Taylor was different. He clearly felt that I was deliberately thrusting deeper into his throat, and he responded with even more enthusiasm. Perhaps it was the tender feeling of his throat that made my body tremble involuntarily. He also felt the tremor and buried his head even deeper. I pushed up forcefully, allowing his mouth to swallow my cock even deeper.

"Oh... mmm... oh, God... oh..." I couldn't help but moan in pleasure.

Maybe it was because there were people present, I became even more depraved. Perhaps watching too much gay porn, scenes like this with multiple people being promiscuous in the bathroom were what I fantasized about. So I didn't care about anything else. Maybe because I made sounds, everyone else stopped and watched us.

One of them said, "Why don't you two go upstairs to have more fun?"

Nick Taylor also stood up and said, "I'm so hot!"

Seeing him exhausted, I told him to take a break.

At this point, he leaned his body against mine and used his hand to tease my nipples, which are a sensitive area for me. Instantly, both of my nipples became hard. He looked at me with a playful smile. Now, I had the opportunity to touch his cock, which was straight and hard, about 17 centimeters long.

I said to him, "It's a shame for such a big cock to go to waste on me."

He replied, "Oh well, as long as it can be put to good use with others."

Actually, I quite liked him. He looked manly and with this big cock, he became even more impressive. If I could accept it, I might really give myself to him.

"How about we go upstairs?" he suggested.

"Okay."

So we got up and left the sauna room.

He said to me, "Wait for me, I'll get a condom from the wardrobe."

After he got the condom, we went upstairs. There weren't many people upstairs, it seemed like only one couple in the corner embracing each other.

He said, "How about we go to a private room?"

"What's there to be afraid of? So many people just did it, why be afraid?" I pulled him towards the last row of resting beds. We lay down and tightly wrapped ourselves together.

"Darling, I really like you," I said.

"Is that so?" he asked.

"Yes, playing with you is so pleasurable."

"Hmph, the real pleasure is yet to come."

We helped each other take off our clothes, touched each other's cocks, and suddenly I had the urge to do a 69 with him. I asked him to turn his head around so we could do a 69. Soon, his hand guided my cock and quickly returned to his warm mouth. This time, he was lying flat, and I thrust my cock down into his mouth from above. With his forceful suction and licking, I quickly regained the feeling. I felt my cock getting harder and the speed and strength of my thrusting increased. His hands were wrapped around my waist, and I quickly began to lick his big cock. I gently licked his glans with my tongue, feeling some moisture on it. I noticed his cock trembling, so I started sucking on his cock.

Occasionally, Nick Taylor would thrust his cock into my mouth, and I didn't back down either. I increased the speed of thrusting into his throat.

Maybe because I was giving him such pleasurable licking, he moaned.

"Oh...oh!...oh...mmh...oh...oh..."

I turned his body over. At this point, I was lying flat and he climbed up to give me a deepthroat. His thick lips, tender flesh, and wet saliva made me feel incredible pleasure.

At that moment, I suddenly discovered that there was also another man lying next to us, watching us.

Damn it, when did he come? I didn't even notice. Whatever, he's just watching on the side, which only enhances the pleasure of my fight.

I gently moved my hand towards Nick Taylor's asshole, and finally touched it. The outer folds were smooth, without any hair. After moistening my finger with lubricant, I slowly entered his body. It was warm inside, not particularly tight. If it's too tight, it's not enjoyable to penetrate. If it's too loose, there's no sensation. I felt that his asshole was just perfect, neither too tight nor too loose. After a slow movement, I inserted another finger and continued moving until Nick Taylor's voice changed from discomfort to pleasure.

At this point, I felt that the time was right, it was time to take action. I turned Nick Taylor over, making him lie flat.

"Be gentle!"

"It's not like it's your first time, why are you scared?"

I spread open Nick Taylor's buttocks, exposing his tender asshole. I used my tongue to lick that asshole, and it was stimulated so wonderfully that it began to contract in excitement. I quickly put on a condom on my dick and applied some lubricant around his asshole. I inserted two fingers and slowly explored his asshole, thrusting in and out. Nick Taylor moaned continuously. When the timing was right, I gently slid my dick into his asshole and began thrusting.

Meanwhile, the man lying beside us had the audacity to touch my undulating butt with one hand and stroke my cock at Nick Taylor's asshole with the other hand.

I felt that his presence would disturb Nick Taylor's involvement, so I angrily said, "Go away."

Seeing that I seemed angry, he didn't dare to touch both of us anymore.

I held onto his legs with both hands and leaned down, slowly kissing him. I felt a warmth, how fortunate it was for men to have the intimacy of skin against skin.

The speed of my thrusts clearly increased. Among them, I didn't forget the straightforward phrase, "Nine shallow, one deep, enhances the soul."

Seeing that he was enjoying it, he said, "Harder, my dear, deeper..."

Seeing him so lewd, I began to thrust deeply and vigorously, and my whole body trembled.

Oh, it felt so good, that friction sensation was fantastic. The greatest pleasure for a man to fuck another man is the penetration of the cock into the asshole.

After fucking for a long time, I had him lift his butt up and entered his body from behind. This doggy-style position is my favorite, because it's the most primal and animalistic.

His tight hole kept gripping my shaft as I thrust in and out. Occasionally, he would unconsciously contract, tightly wrapping around my cock and sending waves of pleasure.

"Oh...it feels so good," he moaned.

"Really?" I asked him.

I don't know how much time had passed, but it felt like we had been playing for too long. I didn't even notice when the person next to us left, but I still didn't feel like coming.

He said, "Let's take a break, I can't take it anymore, you've worn me out."

"Really?"

"Yeah."

So I pulled my cock out of his hole and threw away the condom.

"How about we go downstairs and fuck you in the sauna room?" I suggested.

"Are you crazy?" he looked at me in astonishment.

"It might be exciting, what do you think?"

"Well, okay." He eventually agreed.

We put our clothes back on and went downstairs. After a quick rinse, he led me into a small room next to the sauna room. It was a steam-filled room, very small, with six or seven stools on one side.

We sat down, and he handed me a condom.

I said, "I'm not aroused yet, how am I supposed to put it on?"

He obediently got down and used his mouth to make my cock fully erect again. At this moment, another man entered the room. Knowing that people in the bathhouse liked to watch, we didn't mind. We ignored him and continued with what we were doing. He sat on a stool since it was too dark to see his face.

My cock became even more swollen. I had Nick Taylor hold onto a stool and smoothly put on the condom. Without using lubrication, I plunged all the way in. It wasn't too dry, probably because of what we had fucked earlier, but he still felt a bit uncomfortable. After slowly thrusting a few times, he started moaning. I knew he was feeling good now, so I began to forcefully thrust and fuck him hard.

I fucked him hard, his asshole making a slapping sound as I thrust. He moaned loudly, so I picked up the pace, fucking him harder and deeper, pounding into his core. He started to struggle a bit, asking me to cum faster. Fuck, he was so slutty, and I loved the freedom of sex like this, even with someone else nearby. I fucked him harder, his moans growing louder...

I lifted one of his legs, having him step onto a stool, opening him up even more from behind. Gradually, I increased the intensity of my movements, the sound of our bodies colliding grew louder, like a machine gradually speeding up until it reached its maximum velocity.

"Oh... Oh, God..." With my cries, I thrust harder, releasing my semen, then held onto him tightly.

After taking off the cum-filled condom, I sat on the stool, and had Nick Taylor sit on my lap. I began to stroke his big cock with one hand and play with his nipples with the other. Under the manipulation of my hands, he finally shot his load, a lot of it, making my hands sticky.

"Let's go wash up," I said.

"Yeah."

Finally, the intense battle was over. After we cleaned up and got dressed, we went to another room to sing. It was then that I noticed Monroe, who had come with me, was also singing. Nick Taylor sang really well, with deep emotion, truly captivating me. But I didn't have the courage to pursue any kind of romantic relationship, so I didn't ask for anything.

During the singing session, he realized that I wasn't from City A and asked, "Will you come again in the future?"

"Of course, it's not far from City A," I replied.

"Then give me your phone number."

"Sure."

He kept singing until around 10 o'clock and said he had to go back since he lived with his parents and couldn't stay out overnight. I was reluctant to let him go.

After he got dressed, we exchanged numbers. He told me to come find him in City A when I had time.

Of course, I would find him because being with him was amazing.

Last night, I even texted him, saying I would come find him when I had time. I'm really looking forward to another intimate encounter with him.

Chapter 2 Richard

When it comes to Richard, he was a guy I met in this small northern town in April last year. They say small towns have many stories, and from my perspective, this small town indeed had quite a few. This small town may have retained the peacefulness it had before, but beneath the tranquility, there were hidden currents. First of all, the environment here isn't great, and the roads are irregular. The pace of life is slow, and you often see people leisurely strolling down the streets.

The gay community in this small town can't be compared to the big cities like City A, but it's actually the most prominent place for the LGBTQ+ community in this city, maybe because of the numerous universities located here. The number of gays here is not large, and the quality is varied, but the gays here are wild and uninhibited (at least that's my self-perception).

There are two gay hangouts in this small town, jokingly referred to as Circle B and Circle A.

Circle A seems to be the oldest, just a restroom located in a park, and not many people go there now. Circle B came later, forming as a central street garden after the road reconstruction by the municipal government. For some reason, it became a popular place for the LGBTQ+ community. Especially around 9 pm, there are the most gays here. Although many people come here to dance, you can easily spot gays because their eyes are different.

The gay hangouts are also jokingly referred to as companies, as many people come here to "work" in the evenings. It's called "work" because they come here almost every day. After they arrive, if they don't have a particular target of interest, they usually chat and have fun together. Of course, there are also some individuals who come alone, and they generally prefer not to interact with well-known individuals. They come here occasionally to seek encounters. Compared to restrooms, I think Circle B is relatively better.

When I first came to this small town, I felt like this would be my work and life circle from now on. I couldn't be as carefree as before in unfamiliar cities. After all, the small town was too small, and I might encounter awkward situations. So after coming here, I've been living a quiet life, focusing on my work, and rarely going to online chat rooms because once I enter a chat room, I know I won't be able to control myself from meeting others.

So life passed by peacefully. One day, an online friend on Facebook sent me a message saying, "Let me introduce you to a handsome guy."

This online friend was in his thirties and I had never met him before. But he was well-known in this small town's community and could be considered one of the old-timers. I had always heard that he had a plump figure but was good-natured, perhaps that's why many people enjoyed chatting with him.

After hearing his words, how could I not be intrigued?

I playfully teased him, "Oh, are you playing the role of a matchmaker now?"

"Cut it out, stop joking," he replied.

"I want it, I want it, who said I didn't? But how much does it cost?" I continued jokingly.

"You, why did you ask so. No need cost." he retorted.

I was puzzled. If he wasn't selling, then why did he want to introduce someone to me? So I asked, "Why do you want to introduce him to me?"

"I heard you're new here, so I thought of introducing him to you," he explained.

"Alright, what's his name?" I asked.

He mentioned his online username at that moment, and here we will refer to him as Richard. As soon as I heard the name, I knew who he was. After all, he was quite famous in this community, and I had heard about him before. He seemed to be from a different city but frequented this one, and he appeared to be quite good-looking. If he wasn't attractive, I don't think he would be popular here.

But my overall impression of Richard was that he must be a big shot in this community. If he really was like that, I, being so honest and unable to play games, probably wouldn't be able to handle him.

However, I couldn't resist the temptation and wanted to get in touch with Richard, perhaps due to my own desires. In the end, I managed to contact Richard. During our phone call that afternoon, he said he was going to sing with a group of friends that evening and suggested meeting tomorrow.

The next afternoon, after hastily finishing my work, I called him to ask if he was available.

He humorously replied, "I am, and I'm already in bed."

Upon hearing that, I felt even more convinced that he must be seductive and alluring.

I took a taxi to his place. When he opened the door, he was wearing a translucent underwear, bare-chested, revealing a partially erect member wrapped by the transparent fabric. It looked impressive. Richard indeed looked good, about 185 centimeters tall, slim, fair-skinned, and quite attractive. However, there was always a sense of seductiveness emanating from him.

Once inside, I discovered that he was playing on his computer, video chatting in a chat room.

"Don't be shy, have a seat on the bed," he warmly invited.

At that moment, I glanced around the room. It was messy but felt clean. Clothes and underwear were scattered everywhere on the sofa, and the bedsheet was disheveled, as if some battle had taken place.

"Why do you live here?" I asked.

"It's a friend's place. I came over to hang out and will stay here for a few days. They've gone to work," he explained.

I finally understood that it was someone else's house, and it seemed that the homeowner was also part of the same community.

I sat on the bed, and Richard sat on my thighs facing me. His hands began to wander over my clothes, unbuttoning my jacket button by button. The slow and deliberate movements made me impatient. After removing my jacket, he slid his hands down from my innerwear, grabbing the hem of my shirt and lifting it over my head. Then, he casually tossed my shirt aside and continued hastily undoing my belt and jeans' zipper. Once my belt and zipper were completely undone, Richard's fingers found their way inside my underwear.

Seemingly noticing my arousal, he remarked, "Seems like you're aroused."

"Mm," I was speechless, allowing him to take control.

Suddenly, he forcefully pulled down my underwear and jeans, bringing them all the way down to my ankles. I cooperated by kicking off my shoes, fully unveiling my naked body. And so, I laid bare on the bed.

"Go take a shower," he ordered me, almost as a command.

"Why are you so naughty? Are you teasing me?" I exclaimed. His previous actions had driven me crazy, only to find out that he wanted me to take a shower.

At that moment, he sat down in front of the computer again, chatting with friends online and occasionally standing up to dance.

I entered the bathroom, quickly rinsed off my body, and then lay naked on the bed.

Because of his actions just now, I didn't feel constrained anymore and directly said, "Come over and play."

I lay on the bed, standing naked in front of the boy I liked.

Richard quickly leaned in, kissed me, then moved down my neck, kissing my nipples. His right hand held onto my swollen and erect cock, moving back and forth, helping me masturbate. I couldn't help but start to gasp. His fingers skillfully rubbed my foreskin, constantly flipping it up and down over the glans. I could feel my cock starting to get wet, with big droplets of clear love liquid continuously flowing out from the urethral opening at the tip of the glans.

He moved down along my abdomen and finally reached my glans. When Richard's face was about to touch my plump and swollen glans, he opened his lips and used his tongue to lick the obscene liquid oozing from the urethral opening. Then his tongue closely followed the sensitive frenulum beneath my glans, moving from bottom to top, scraping and licking towards his urethral opening. When his tongue reached the raised flesh peak on top of the glans, it once again retraced its path and continued licking. This is the most sensitive area on a man's cock, and Richard started off by giving me such wild stimulation. Under Richard's intense stimulation, I excitedly moaned, with a very satisfied and pleased expression on my face.

Richard began to engulf my glans in his mouth, forcefully opening his jaw and taking it in. After he swallowed my glans, his lips wrapped around the large shaft just behind the glans. Richard's lips tightened slightly and began moving up and down. The friction between his tongue and my glans felt incredibly enjoyable, and I was starting to struggle with this immense pleasure and stimulation.

I pressed him down under me, biting his raised and erect cock with my mouth, licking his urethral opening with my tongue, watching as it secreted a bit of shiny liquid. I greedily sucked on his cock, feeling an incredibly sweet taste. His expression in my eyes became more and more alluring and captivating. I lifted his legs up high and carefully licked his anus with the tip of my tongue. His anus started to contract, seeming to anticipate something.

I took out some lubricant and applied it around his anus, also smearing some on my condom.

"I'm ready to enter," I said.

"Be gentle," he replied.

I spread his legs apart and positioned my cock against his tight anus, slowly pushing it in.

He said, "Don't move for a moment, it's a bit painful."

I teased, "Even experienced people can feel pain?"

But I didn't move, letting my member stay inside him for a few seconds. He then used his hands to signal me to continue, so I held onto his legs and thrust forcefully. I penetrated his tight hole, feeling the spasms and contractions of his smooth intestinal walls. It felt like he was grabbing onto the sheets as his anus and rectum clenched tightly around me, creating an intense sensation that made me not want to move.

Gradually, his tension eased and I descended from my peak. I couldn't help but start moving, wanting to conquer Richard, who was incredibly seductive. I flipped Richard over and made him assume a doggy-style position. I gripped his slim and firm waist tightly, pressing down almost to the bedsheet, lifting his buttocks high and fully exposing his anus. With my cock, I deliberately rubbed against his anal opening, causing him to cry out, "It's so itchy."

At this moment, we both enjoyed it. I guided my member inside until it was fully inserted, and he couldn't help but let out a scream. Watching my swollen member thrusting in and out of his pink hole, it was an incredibly pleasurable sight. I moved with vigor, feeling each thrust venturing into a mysterious territory within his body, making me want to go deeper.

After a while, I pulled him to the edge of the bed and had him lie down while I stood on the floor, spreading his legs apart and thrusting vigorously.

Time passed, and Richard began to stroke his own member with his hand.

"Let's climax together," he said.

His hand movements became faster, and I was approaching the peak of pleasure. At this moment, I held onto Richard's legs tightly and forcefully pushed my member into the depths of his anus. I ejaculated the accumulated essence for a long time, the hot streams rushing into his body.

He knew I had climaxed and said, "Don't pull out, I'm close too."

Richard frantically stroked his own member, letting out loud moans that made me worried someone might hear. Alongside his loud exclamations, he also reached his climax, ejaculating milky white semen in spurts onto his chest.

"Damn, it's intense. You shot so much, so far," I said.

"It's all because of you," he said in a coquettish tone.

After the sex, the two of us lay exhausted on the bed.

I said, "I won't forget the passion with you."

"Oh, you probably say that to everyone," he replied.

"No, it's not true. How could it be?"

Afterward, we chatted for a while. I was afraid the owner of the room would come back, so I left.

Honestly, in this small town, I never encountered him again or anyone else who drove me crazy and fascinated me like he did. Making love with me might be ordinary for him, but for me, it was truly unforgettable. Regardless of his situation, I wish him a safe and happy life, always.

Chapter 3 Thomas

This is a northern city, where too many memories remain, making it hard for me to know where to begin recollecting.

From the moment I stepped into this circle, to when I graduated from college and came to this city for postgraduate studies, it was only then that I truly came into contact with the LGBT community. Upon my arrival here, I learned online that the LGBT community in this city is quite popular, with various groups, such as Boy's Love and Blue Circle, standing out.

The Boy's Love group is vast, and the one I directly clashed with was their leader. This Boy's Love leader, named Vito, I'm not entirely sure about his age, but he seemed fairly young. He was known for being fierce and had a big reputation in the community, as no one dared to challenge him directly. By chance, in a chat room, for some unknown reason, we ended up arguing, and the argument escalated. In the end, he left me with these words, "Wait, don't let me catch you."

Fate has its unexpected twists, and it seems that it was just a coincidence.

One evening, I was at an internet café near the school, wondering why I chose this particular place. It was because this internet café was located near a gathering spot for the LGBT community. At that time, this spot was bustling, with countless people coming and going from a small restroom. There were also many people walking around the area.

Another reason for choosing this internet café was that the café's administrator was also part of the community. He was a bit chubby but had a fierce reputation; though I heard he was a good person. I didn't come to this internet café because of him; it was more because many of the LGBT people I knew frequented this place. I was only there to see these people, without any other intentions.

That night, while I was browsing the internet, a person came out from another room. As he was about to leave, he possibly noticed that I was in the chat room and realized that I was also a member of the LGBT community. Boldly, he sat next to me. He saw that my chat room name was "Passionate Nude Guy," which shocked him.

He asked me, "Are you Passionate Nude Guy?"

Taken aback by his question, I looked at him for the first time. He was tall, with a somewhat slim figure, wearing a black shoulder-hugging shirt and black pants.

I straightforwardly replied, "Yes, that's me. What's up?"

"Do you know who I am?" he countered, "Come out with me for a moment."

I genuinely didn't recognize him, so I said, "Why should I go out with you? What's the matter?"

He sternly said to me, "Just come out, let me talk to you about something."

At the time, I thought it was something serious. It was only after going outside that I realized he was indeed the legendary leader of Boy's Love, Vito. I was completely startled. I asked him, "What do you want from me?"

At that time, the young boy with him was his boyfriend, Wright. I heard he had just turned 18, but he was tall, good-looking, and quite masculine (I won't go into the details of my story with him here).

Wright kindly said, "It's okay, don't be afraid of him."

With Wright saying that, I found myself liking this guy, Vito.

I can't remember exactly what Vito said at the time; I guess he just told me not to argue with him casually in the future. After that, he didn't seem hostile anymore, settled his bill at the internet cafe, and quickly returned to school.

Looking back now, I realize my courage was quite small at the time. After all, I had just started getting involved in this community and didn't know much about the situation within it.

That's how I came into contact with a large family in this city, Boy's Love. As for the bottoms in Boy's Love, I also came into contact with a few of them. But the most frequent interaction was with Jack and a few others.

Jack used to be a member of the Boy's Love family, but due to some reason, he had a falling out and left. Jack was also a well-known figure in the community. It was him and a group of friends who took me to the Blue Club. Since being with them at the club, I started to become a bit more unrestrained.

I remember my first time at the club, it was exciting and curious. The club wasn't only filled with LGBTQ+ individuals; it seemed like everyone agreed to come here on Friday nights. The people going to the club, some dressed flamboyantly, some revealing, I even saw a guy wearing a crop top; while dancing, some had fans, some had handkerchiefs; under the chaotic lights, they all danced like demons. What stood out in my memory was a very petite boy dancing near the cages on stage, with graceful movements, a handsome face, and very likable.

Here, Jack told me who the members of the Blue Circle were. After that, I also learned about the Blue Circle. It is said that the members of the Blue Circle are all handsome guys, very outstanding. Those who don't look good can only be servants or something like that within the Blue Circle, but I'm not sure about the specifics; it's all hearsay. There are also rumors that some boys in the Blue Circle are money boys, which made me feel that the people in the Blue Circle should all be good-looking. Later, I found out that Thomas is the leader of the Blue Circle.

At the club, I also saw Thomas. He had a bright appearance, short hair, a tall and lean figure. He was dressed impeccably, and his tight-fitting clothes accentuated his slender physique, giving off a very pleasing feeling. Handsome guys are meant to be admired from afar and not played with. Although I liked him in my heart, as someone as timid as me back then, how could I have a one-night experience with him? That was the first time I saw Thomas.

After one year, during the summer vacation, I returned to school early from home. At that time, I was the only one in the dormitory. I spent my days surfing the internet at night and sleeping during the day, enjoying my life. It was during this time that I started chatting with Thomas in a chat room (I didn't know at the time that he was the leader of the Blue Circle).

I still remember when Thomas asked me if I was a "Top" or a "Bottom". I specifically told him, "I've only been involved in these matters for about a year, and before that, it was more like a '69' situation."

Thinking back to the topic of being a 'Top' or a 'Bottom' now, I feel regretful, giving my virginity to a person around 30 years old who wasn't someone I liked.

One evening, feeling bored, I went to the place not far from our school that was mentioned earlier, the restroom. It was late, so there were hardly any people around.

At that spot, I walked around aimlessly, and at that moment, a man around 30 years old approached and asked, "What time is it?"

People who have been to many meeting points, such as the park by the river in this city, would often approach and ask, "What time is it?" This phrase became a typical way to identify fellow LGBTQ+ individuals.

He was around 185 cm tall, not in great shape anymore, wore glasses, and had a genteel appearance. After exchanging a few words with him, seeing that I was a student, and probably didn't have any place to go, he invited me to his place.

Since there was nobody around the meeting point, and I wanted to release my pent-up emotions, I went along with him. When I arrived at his place, I found out that he wasn't married and lived with his mother. It was probably late, as his mother had already gone to sleep. We quietly entered his room.

As soon as we entered the room, he hugged me, tearing off my clothes with his big hands. Looking at my athletic body, he got excited, holding me and letting his big hands roam freely on my body. I felt a tingling sensation with every touch.

"Let's go to bed, I want to love you properly," he said, kissing me.

I have to admit, he was really skilled in bed. I would say he was the best I've ever encountered in terms of technique.

He effortlessly placed me on the bed and covered me. His lips quickly pressed against mine, initiating a passionate and intense kiss. Under his vigorous assault, I could hardly resist. He kissed my neck and trailed along my hairline, his gentle lips feeling like raindrops on my skin. In that instant, my mind anxiously flooded with countless strange and peculiar questions - how should I cooperate with him?

Lost in my pleasure, he caressed my body while his hand ventured between my legs, lightly teasing my cock, causing me to involuntarily moan. Then his lips descended onto my belly button, continuously licking it, the tingling sensation nearly intoxicating me. What drove me to the edge was when he turned my body over and suddenly his tongue glided over my anus. It had never been so stimulating there, and in that moment, I had a slight desire to be penetrated.

Then, he flipped my body back to face him, and his sturdy body pressed closer to mine. Lowering his head, he enclosed my member with his mouth, flicking his tongue over it, gently massaging my entire glans, not neglecting my frenulum. He began an up and down motion, as his tongue reached into my urethral opening, an unprecedented trembling sensation crawled up my entire genitals. I felt the pleasure about to pour down like a storm.

I murmured, "Don't."

He paid no attention to me, continuing to stimulate me. Waves of pleasure washed over me, reaching the utmost satisfaction. In that moment, I truly wished time could stand still.

"Do you want me to fuck my asshole?"

"Fuck asshole? I haven't done that before," I replied to him.

"Really?" he said, half doubtful.

"Yes."

"Give it a try, if it's uncomfortable, we can stop," he said. "But it will definitely give you pleasure."

Hearing him say that, I nodded. Maybe it was because the way he had pleasured me with his tongue earlier felt so good, I lost control and decided to give him my first time.

He got some shower gel and applied it to my manhood, and he applied a lot to his anus as well. It seemed like he inserted a few fingers, maybe to make it more lubricated inside. Then he climbed onto the bed, but as I tried to insert myself from behind while supporting my manhood with my hand, I couldn't seem to find the right position. It either couldn't go in or went between his legs. I was getting anxious.

He told me, "Don't rush, take it slow."

I felt that it wasn't comfortable for him to be lying down like that, so I asked him to raise his buttocks. This way, his anus was presented in front of me, surrounded by a silky bath gel, giving off a shiny appearance. I held onto his waist with one hand and my manhood with the other, pressing against his anus. Just as I was about to thrust forcefully, he seemed to purposely relax his backside, and I easily pushed my entire manhood inside.

"Stay still for now, slowly ease in," he immediately exclaimed.

Perhaps due to it being my first time, I may have been overly rash.

After keeping my manhood inside his anus for a while, I began gently moving it back and forth. At that point, I was covered in sweat, unsure if it was because of excitement or nervousness.

At that moment, I thought my manhood felt comfortable inside him, enveloped by his tender walls. My glans seemed particularly sensitive. I gradually increased the speed and intensity, and he softly moaned. Seeing him like that, I suddenly wondered if it really felt this good as a Bottom. Within no time, I felt the most amazing sensation of orgasm in my life, warm and viscous fluid shooting into his small hole.

That's how I experienced the joy of anal sex for the first time, giving myself to this polite and cultured man in his thirties. That night, he showed me that men can also have such wonderful sexual experiences with each other.

The topic should shift to something formal, let's talk about Thomas.

After making plans with Thomas in the chat room that night, I waited for him in my dormitory. In no time, he said he had arrived, so I quickly went downstairs to meet him at the school gate.

When I saw him, I was surprised and asked him, "Are you Thomas?"

"No," he replied.

"Don't lie to me, I've seen you at Blue Club."

"Oh," he remained silent.

He came on a motorcycle, just as neat and tidy as before, full of vitality, and dressed very nicely, giving off a sense of competence. I brought him to our school and after parking his motorcycle downstairs in the dormitory building, we entered my dormitory.

I lived in a dormitory with two bunk beds, housing only four people and having four desks. On one side, there was a small shelf similar to a bookshelf; it was actually just a thin piece of wood, so the dormitory next to ours was almost connected. We didn't have to go over to talk or greet each other. Often at night, lying in bed, the two dormitories would start chatting.

Because it was my first time having sex with a man in the dormitory, I was worried that the dormitory next door would hear us, which made me quite anxious, but also excited, with an irresistible feeling.

We stood in the room, embracing each other tightly, pressing our bodies together. Before long, both of our lower bodies reacted, becoming aroused almost simultaneously, rubbing against each other through our jeans.

Thomas put his tongue in my mouth, and I had no choice but to intertwine with him. Generally, I rarely kiss anyone, and even less often with tongue. He pulled down my jeans and his hand slipped into my underwear, gently gripping my manhood. I also pulled down his jeans, finally revealing his buttocks. I only realized when I touched it that he was wearing a thong, a very thin strap encircling his anus.

I asked him, "Is it comfortable to wear this?"

He said it was quite comfortable, sometimes feeling a pleasant sensation from the constriction on the anus.

We looked at each other and smiled.

We quickly stripped off all our clothes. When I looked at him, his figure was really slim, without a trace of excess fat. We held each other tightly, his waist lightly swaying, our erections rubbing against each other, creating a wonderful sensation. Soon, we were both fully aroused.

We touched our glans together, rubbing against each other, moistening each other's manhood with the fluids we produced.

We immersed ourselves in this wonderful game of desire, gradually becoming more and more passionate. His movements started to become rougher, and I knew he was burning with desire, so I let him take control.

Sometimes, I wasn't very proactive, but I enjoyed being the one taken in charge. I lay flat on the bed, and because it was in the dormitory and the bed was small, he had to crawl on top of me, his whole body pressing against mine, passionately kissing me. I was also aroused by him, responding to him intensely.

His lips touched every inch of my skin, leaving a trail of kisses. At the same time, his lower body kept rubbing against my cock, and I moved my waist with him, entwining with each other.

I kept rubbing my legs against his body and crossed them tightly behind him, holding him tightly. He kissed down my body, his lips lingering around my belly button and groin, but deliberately avoiding my cock. I impatiently craved his touch, but he teased me on purpose.

He seemed to sense my impatience and turned his body, assuming a 69 position with me. He took my long-desired manhood into his mouth and gently sucked on it. I also stuffed his cock into my mouth, savoring it with abandon. We were both enveloped in each other's warmth, pleasure flowing through our bodies.

I didn't hold back either. My tongue licked around his glans, cock, and scrotum, occasionally taking his testicles into my mouth. Meanwhile, my restless hands reached behind him, caressing his anus and then inserting my index finger to stir it, making his body tremble constantly, expressing to me his enjoyment of the sensation.

He passionately took my cock into his mouth, and I indulged in his touch, trying to bring him as much pleasure as possible. Meanwhile, my fingers kept thrusting into Thomas' anus, starting with one finger, then adding the middle one, and finally inserting the ring finger as well. The three fingers moved in different directions inside, and I could feel that he not only accepted it but was experiencing immense pleasure.

Now it was time for me to enter his body. I said to him, "I'm going in."

Because the bed was too small and there was an upper bunk, there was no way to stand straight or maneuver properly. So I got off the bed, stood on the ground, turned him sideways, and placed a pillow under his buttocks. I pressed his legs and spread them as wide as possible. I applied some lubricant around his anus, then used the head of my cock to tease it, rubbing against it. Unable to resist my teasing, he moaned and urged me to penetrate him quickly.

After playing around for a while and seeing that he couldn't resist any longer, I aimed my glans at his anus and pushed forward with force. My cock easily plunged deep into his tight hole.

"...Oh...Oh, my God!" He couldn't help but let out a loud moan.

When he moaned, it scare me, and I said, "Be quiet, the people next door will hear."

I was afraid the people next door could hear us.

In fact, I was really excited. I wanted him to moan loudly, but I was also afraid of the people next door hearing us. This stimulated me even more, and I thrust harder and faster, rapidly pounding his tight little hole, feeling the friction of his soft and tender walls against my glans and cock. I looked down at Thomas; he closed his eyes, furrowed his brows, and started to let out soft moans. With each thrust, his moans grew louder. Sometimes I had to remind him to keep his voice down.

We went on for a long time, and then he asked me to sit on the bed while he positioned himself on top. Due to the upper bunk, he was afraid of hitting his head, so I sat on a chair instead. This allowed him to sit on my cock, assuming a more dominant position. He passionately moved his ass up and down on my big cock, impaling himself deeply each time, letting my cock penetrate deep inside him. To be honest, I wasn't a big fan of this position because it didn't feel as pleasurable to me. I couldn't freely exert myself; instead, I let the other person control the speed and depth. But this time was different. I held onto his waist, and he moved up and down smoothly, tightly rubbing against me with each motion.

He seemed a bit tired and suggested changing positions. So I had him turn around, holding onto the chair while I attacked from behind. Gripping onto his slim waist, I thrust forward with force, completely entering his body once again, and then started to thrust rapidly. I don't know why that day I was so vigorous, becoming more and more intense without any signs of climaxing.

After who knows how long he made me lie back on the bed again, still in the same position, and I attacked him vigorously. My cock was throbbing with passion, almost ready to explode.

I increased the frequency of my thrusts, and his body seemed to respond to me as he softly uttered, "Oh... oh..."

A hot liquid gushed into his body. At that moment, he didn't let me pull out my cock. He increased the pace of his hand job, and soon a stream of white fluid sprayed out, shooting several times. After he finished, I pulled out my cock, and along with it, some of the semen flowed out. It was an extremely depraved scene.

This passionate encounter exhausted both of us, but the pleasure of sex far outweighed the exhaustion in our bodies. After cleaning ourselves up with tissues, we embraced and lay on my tiny bed for a while. It was uncomfortable to have two people in one bed, so he went to sleep on my classmate's bed.

Until the next day when he left, I was still immersed in the sexual bliss of the previous night.

It has been nearly two years since I left that city. Searching through my memories, the clearest one is probably of Thomas. Here, I wish my sexual partner, Thomas, happiness. Even though the next time we meet, he may not remember that passionate encounter we had.

Chapter 4 Leif

Later, I met Leif in City W. It was during summer vacation when my gay friend Oliver invited me to his house to hang out.

I actually met Oliver in an online chat room, but I don't remember the exact reason why. Maybe it was because we had been chatting online for a long time, and it had been a while since we last saw each other, so we had a lot of expectations for each other.

Eventually, we did meet up, and I remember vividly that he was wearing a white tank top, blue and white jeans, and white sneakers that day. Oliver had fair skin and messy hair, and if I had to describe him in two words, it would be "sunshine."

Oliver was a sophomore at the time and loved swimming. So we had a common hobby. We would often swim together at our school's swimming pool. He was one of those flirty boys. When we got tired and rested by the poolside, he would look around to see if there were any attractive guys nearby. If he spotted someone he liked, he would purposely swim over and strike up a conversation.

Oliver was adorable, with no pretense at all. He was genuine when spending time with friends and never pretended to be someone he wasn't. Another thing he liked to do was observe good-looking guys walking on the street. If an attractive guy passed by, he would carefully watch them for a while and then say, "He must also be gay."

That's how our relationship began. We spent time together either swimming or going shopping and eating out. One day at noon, Oliver sent me a text message asking me to go swimming with him. Unfortunately, I couldn't leave, so we didn't meet until after 4 PM at the entrance of the swimming pool. Like usual, we swam together and then went to a small sushi restaurant we often frequented.

During the meal, he looked at me with seriousness and softly said, "Why don't you take things further with me?"

"Further? What do you mean?" I asked.

"Do you really not want to have sex with me?" he asked.

"I have thought about it," I replied. "But we are friends, and if friends sleep together, it might ruin the long-lasting friendship we have."

This has always been my belief. In my perspective, if two good friends engage in sex, it might create a lack of attraction and make the pure friendship unstable.

"How about we give it a try?" he stared at me and said.

"Are you sure about that? Once we do it, there's no turning back. Don't say I took advantage of you," I warned.

"Who's taking advantage of whom is still uncertain," he said.

Finally, we decided to book a hotel room. We went to a hotel not far from our school, afraid that the receptionist would notice something strange.

As soon as we entered the room, Oliver came over and hugged me. I told him it was still early, so we should take a shower first. I went in to shower, and he would occasionally come in and ask to shower together. However, the shower area in this hotel was not particularly spacious, so we couldn't shower together, which was a pity.

Oliver came out of the bathroom, wiped his wet face with a towel, shook his body a few times, and his erect cock followed suit, vigorously shaking. It was at that moment that I realized Oliver's cock wasn't long, but it was thick.

Looking at Oliver's muscular body, with such smooth and tender skin, giving it a firm squeeze felt incredibly elastic. It was a mix of softness and hardness. I couldn't help but imagine thrusting my own hard cock into him right away.

The real play was just beginning. I moved my hand towards the erect, bulging cock in front of me. Oliver couldn't hold it back anymore and let out a soft moan of "oh."

I held the base of Oliver's cock with a towel ring in my fist and slowly slid towards the swollen, rosy glans. When my hand was about halfway there, Oliver's anus slowly opened its small, cherry-like mouth, and a shiny drop of fluid dripped out.

I gently teased his anus with my tongue, then took his entire large glans into my mouth. My tongue inside my mouth continuously teased the sensitive glans like an electric current. Unable to resist the tingling sensation, he pushed his hard cock forward, entering my mouth fully. I didn't particularly enjoy giving oral sex to others, so at that moment, I felt a bit nauseous.

I used my mouth and hands together, playing with it for a while, occasionally glancing up at Oliver, who was moaning with his head thrown back. Oliver began to twist his tense body.

At this point, I let go of the cock in my mouth and lifted Oliver's legs. He cooperated and lifted his legs along with my guidance, exposing his round and jade-like buttocks. I lightly touched Oliver's recently washed and tender anus with my saliva-drenched fingers.

"Oh," Oliver trembled all over from this sudden teasing, his moans growing louder and more lascivious.

Seeing his reaction, I began to rapidly move my middle finger back and forth,directly thrusting it into Oliver. He continuously emitted trembling moans, enjoying the pleasure of my finger rubbing against his soft and tender inner walls.

After a few thrusts, I let go of his legs and positioned myself to enter his mouth with my own erect cock. Oliver opened his lips wide, eagerly swallowing and tasting it.

After a few rounds of swallowing, he turned his body around and positioned himself on top of me. He quickly straddled me, holding my cock with his hands, ready to enter his tight hole.

"No need condom?" I asked him.

"Did you buy condoms?" he responded.

At that moment, I remembered that I hadn't bought any condoms.

He said, "Don't worry, I haven't been as a Bottom many times."

He sat down on me suddenly, his movement was slow, and his expression was somewhat menacing, perhaps because he wasn't accustomed to it. His anus was still quite tight. After a few up and down movements, I felt uncomfortable underneath. I sat up, held him, and laid him down on the bed. He lay back, lifted his legs high with his hands, revealing his round buttocks and pink anus.

Watching his anus open and close, I applied some lubricant to Oliver's anus. I rubbed my thick finger against the tight opening several times, then inserted my index finger into him, circling and stroking a few times. I teased his anus, making it itch, and he started to moan.

"You're so slutty," I said.

Seeing Oliver's lustful appearance, I felt extremely excited. I pulled out my finger that was squeezed by his anus, held my own erect cock, and thrust it into Oliver's tight asshole.

Thrusting against his anus, slowly moving my cock back and forth, Oliver began to relax a bit, coordinating his breathing. He started contracting and expanding with my thrusting motion, gradually stretching his anal muscles, and slowly taking my glans into his asshole. Once my glans passed the tight muscle, the rest would go smoothly. Generally, the coronal ridge of the glans is the thickest part of the cock, so as long as this thickest part passed through, the rest could easily enter and exit the tight hole.

Then, I suddenly pulled out my entire cock and quickly lowered my head to see the red and tender hole that my cock had stretched open in Oliver. It was gaping wetly, as if it didn't know what had happened, with its opening wide open.

Watching the pink hole slowly closing up, and seeing Oliver completely losing himself, constantly squirming, I abruptly thrust my waist and hips, my cock penetrating Oliver's body, quickly thrusting in and out of his tight asshole, feeling the friction between my glans and the soft and tender inner walls.

I looked down at Oliver's face, his eyes closed, eyebrows furrowed tightly, and he began to let out soft moans. As the speed of my thrusting increased, his moans grew louder.

At the same time, he started jerking off with one hand, his speed getting faster and faster. As he sped up, his anus involuntarily contracted. Along with his contractions, I felt myself approaching the point of no return. The thrusting became smaller and faster, and I also began to moan loudly.

"I'm going to cum, oh... oh, my God..." he shouted.

Just as the words fell, a white stream of semen sprayed out vigorously, shooting far. With Oliver's warm and tender walls tightly enveloping my cock, as his climax approached, my own orgasm, already on the brink of collapse, became even more difficult to control. Finally, at that moment, it burst forth, my semen spraying wildly, and I couldn't even pull out in time.

"Oh, that was amazing, baby," I said to him.

At that moment, he held me tightly, making me feel happy, even though I understood that happiness was only temporary. But I still felt that moment was worth remembering.

The next morning, he woke me up by touching my cock. Under his stimulation, we had sex again before going back to school.

During that period of time, we were often together, occasionally booking hotel rooms and living a joyful life, playing without a care. That summer vacation, he invited me to come to his hometown, City W, and the temperature there in summer was much more comfortable than here. So, two months later, I took a train alone and endured more than 10 hours of shaking to finally reunite with Oliver in City W.

Oliver brought me to his home.

After putting down our luggage, he said, "You've been on the train all night. Let me take you to shower."

So, he and I went to a bathhouse not far from his home. There, after I showered, as soon as I lay down in a private room, he pounced on me, saying he wanted to give me a kiss. I suggested we go back home quickly instead, where we could do anything we wanted.

That afternoon, we had sex at his house, and in the evening, he said he wanted to take me to a club.

At night, Oliver and I went to the club to dance. The owner of the club was also part of our circle. When we entered, I went to the restroom, and when I came out, I saw Oliver talking to two friends.

I walked over, and Oliver introduced me, "This is David, a friend I've known for a long time, and this is his boyfriend, Leif."

Then he introduced me to them.

David, probably around 29 years old, had short hair and darker skin, with thick eyebrows and not small eyes. He wore a white T-shirt and blue jeans, and had long shoes. He looked quite well-built and very manly. I thought he probably had abs, and maybe his cock was also large.

David's boyfriend, Leif, was probably around 23 years old. He had longer hair and fair skin, with a slender figure. He carried a big bag and had a more feminine dressing style, but I didn't think he was too flamboyant. He could be considered a sunny and cheerful boy. I was particularly attracted to this type, but unfortunately, he already had a boyfriend. Otherwise, there might have been some exciting encounters.

Since we all knew each other, after we entered the club, we sat together. After ordering drinks, people were already dancing on the dance floor.

At that moment, Leif pulled David to dance, and David looked at me and said, "Wait a bit, we just got here, no need to rush."

I was confused. He replied to his boyfriend while looking at me.

Leif insisted on pulling him to dance, and Oliver said, "Let's go dance together."

Leif turned back to David and said, "Stay put, don't wander off everywhere."

After Leif and Oliver left, only David and I were left. We exchanged greetings, but I can't remember the specifics.

Suddenly, he asked me, "Do you like guys like me?"

"Of course. Where can I find such a handsome man?"

"Really?" he asked in return.

Indeed, I liked men like him, very manly men. Occasionally, I would wonder what it would feel like to be a bottom. But that was just a fleeting thought because it was hard for me to accept it physically and psychologically.

I said to him, "I do like you, but we have a conflict."

"Haha..." he laughed.

He leaned close to my ear and said, "How do you know I don't bottom?"

Hearing him say that, I was surprised and delighted. I didn't expect that such a manly man could also be a bottom.

"Is it really possible?" I asked him.

"Yes."

"Aren't you afraid of your boyfriend finding out?"

"I'll just hide it from him. Besides, you won't be staying here all the time."

I thought about it, and when I leave, we won't be in contact anymore, so his boyfriend probably won't suspect anything.

"What about when he's around? How can we do it?"

"After I send him home at night, I'll come find you."

"Do you know his old house?"

"I do."

At that moment, Leif and Oliver happened to walk over.

Leif was already sweating a lot and complained to David in a spoiled manner, "Help me wipe my sweat."

David smiled and winked at me, then wiped the sweat off Leif.

At that moment, we suddenly heard a chubby lady on the stage shout, "Everyone, quiet down. Now, let's welcome the beautiful Miss Angel to the stage."

A seductive woman walked onto the stage. Later, after the chubby lady introduced her, I learned that Miss Angel was actually a trans woman. I had never seen a trans woman before, she looked quite beautiful from a distance.

The stage and the crowd were lively. I stood up to go to the restroom and asked who would come with me. I originally intended to ask David, but unexpectedly, Leif said he wanted to go.

As soon as we entered the restroom and saw no one around, Leif said, "Hey handsome, where are you staying tonight?"

"Oh, I'm staying at Oliver's old place."

"Really? Is Oliver your sugar daddy?"

"Don't joke around. We're just good friends," I defended myself. In reality, I just didn't want them to know about my involvement with Oliver, afraid that it might affect him in the future since they all lived in the same city.

"That sounds boring. How about I accompany you tonight?"

When Leif said that, it surprised me even more than hearing what David said earlier. I thought to myself, surely they wouldn't be up to something.

"If your boyfriend finds out, I won't survive. I can't steal someone's love," I said.

"He won't find out. I don't live with him. I'll come find you later, okay, handsome?"

He said that, making me feel uneasy. So I said, "How about tomorrow during the day? I danced so much tonight and I need a good night's sleep. I won't go out tomorrow during the day."

Upon hearing me say that, he didn't insist and said, "Alright, give me your phone number now."

I told him my number and asked him to call me later in the morning.

We returned to the dance hall where Miss Angel was still performing on stage.

We kept playing until around midnight. We left the club together, and Oliver said he wanted to get some late-night snacks. After eating, it was already very late. David and Leif left when we did, and as they were leaving, David intentionally winked at me. We both knew what it meant.

So I told Oliver that he should stay at his new place tonight.

He asked, "What do you mean?"

I knew I couldn't hide it from him, and there was no other way to convince him, so I told him, "David wants to hook up with me."

"Damn, did you make plans?"

"Yes," I said.

After he sent his boyfriend home, he came to find me.

"Damn, you're heartless, cheating on him in front of his face."

"It's not my fault, he seduced me."

"Fine."

Seeing Oliver agree, I felt relieved. I was afraid he wouldn't leave, and then I wouldn't be able to have sex with the very manly David.

After returning to Oliver's old place alone, I freshened up and got into bed. I had no idea how much time had passed and started wondering if David had stood me up, when I heard a knocking on the door.

I got up and opened the door, only to find that it was David.

"What took you so long?" he asked.

"Oh, I went back again, washed up," I replied.

"Are you working tomorrow?" he asked.

"Yes," I answered.

"Then let's sleep early," he said.

David and I walked into the bedroom. Once inside, we lay on the soft bed. He touched me over my underwear for a while before finally taking them off.

"Your shaft looks beautiful, so straight," he said.

"What about yours? Let me see!" I went straight to groping his cock through his pants. It wasn't erect yet, but already quite large.

"Hurry up and take off your clothes," I urged him.

He held my cock in his hand, and I also gripped his. His cock wasn't very big, but it was a bit thick.

He asked me, "Can you give me a blowjob?"

"Of course!" I said and proceeded to take his cock into my mouth, all the way to the base, and then sucked hard.

"Oh, you suck so well, it feels amazing. Go deeper."

I sucked his cock vigorously while reaching out my hands to caress his upper body, stroking his firm chest and pinching his erect nipples. His moans grew louder. As I moved my hands down, he actually has abs.

David and I switched positions, going into a 69 position, and he eagerly took my shaft into his mouth.

After around 5 minutes, my cheeks were getting sore, and David shouted, "It feels so good, I'm about to cum."

Hearing him say that, I quickly pulled his member out of my mouth.

"Damn, you can't cum so early. The best part is still to come," I said.

Then I had David lie on the bed, raise his hips, and I used my hand to draw circles around his anus. I lightly applied some lubricant and then gently teased his anus, causing his tender flesh to occasionally protrude, resulting in rhythmic contractions. It seemed like he was anticipating something.

Seeing David's hips starting to move and hearing his moans, I inserted one finger gently into his anus. It was hot and smooth inside, and when I reached deep inside, I could clearly feel David's tightening. Slowly, I added another finger. Actually, I didn't find David's anus to be very tight; I was just concerned about him feeling pain, so I gently let him adjust. Finally, all three fingers could enter, and I knew it was about time.

"Hey, are you really a top? Why isn't it very tight back there?" I asked him.

"Damn, why are you asking that? Just insert your shaft already," he said, "Hurry up!"

I knew my fingers had already aroused him to the point of desire.

I had David lie flat on the bed, placed a pillow under his hips, and took out a bottle of lubricant. I applied some to my shaft and also smeared some on his anus. Then I lifted his legs and pressed my glans against his anus. Because of the lubricant, with a gentle push, my entire cock entered David's anus.

After I enter the other person, I don't immediately start thrusting to allow them to adjust. I would lower my head and kiss them, say some words, or even stick my tongue into their ear and lick it. This makes the other person's anus automatically relax, not forcefully contracting due to the previous insertion. In fact, it's a tactic to make the other person relax their guard, allowing me to thrust vigorously and quickly.

Similarly, I gently extended my tongue into his ear, and he immediately moaned in response. At this point, I could freely move in and out, thrusting my shaft deep inside, then pulling it back one-third and forcefully thrusting it back in.

"Oh! You're squeezing me so tight, it feels amazing! I have to fuck you to death," I exclaimed loudly while gasping for breath.

"Is that so? I'm also too comfortable. Fuck me hard! I love it so much."

I couldn't believe my eyes. Despite having such a masculine appearance, when lying on the bed and being fucked, he had such a debauched look.

Hearing his words, it aroused me even more, and I vigorously thrust into his anus like a raging motor.

Our lustful cries mixed with the sounds of our lovemaking filled the entire room.

Later, we changed positions multiple times: doggy style, side position (he laid on his side while I faced him and penetrated him, allowing me to fuck him while also being able to lean down and suck his nipple), and more.

After a while, I increased the speed of my thrusts, yelling, "Oh, I'm going to cum, I can't hold it anymore, oh!"

I abruptly pulled out my cock from David's anus, aimed it at his body, and vigorously stroked it with my hand.

With a shudder and two lewd moans of "Oh, Oh!"

A large amount of semen sprayed out like bullets, most of it landing on David's chest, with some on his face.

After wiping the semen off his face with tissue paper, I asked, "How do you want to ejaculate?"

He replied, "You want me to do it again?"

"I told you when I was dancing, I won't be a Bottom."

"Then help me ejaculate orally."

To be honest, after I ejaculated, I didn't have the energy to serve others anymore, nor the interest to give oral sex.

But the man beside me fascinated me a bit, so I reluctantly agreed. However, he ejaculated quickly too, under the dual action of my mouth and hand. It didn't take him more than 10 minutes.

After tidying up, we got into bed to sleep.

I asked him, "Do you often sneak out behind your boyfriend's back to fool around with others?"

He said, "No, there are only a few people in City W. If I were to fool around with someone else, he would find out sooner or later."

"Just focus on your relationship with your boyfriend, don't be too promiscuous."

I felt conflicted at that moment. Why didn't I advise him to treat his boyfriend well before we had sex? Why did I only do it afterwards? I was quite cunning, haha.

We chatted about various topics for a while, then he held me tightly as we fell into a deep sleep.

The next morning around 8 o'clock, David got up and prepared for the day.

After finishing his morning routine, he said to me, "I have to leave now."

"Give me a kiss, dear."

He pecked my face abruptly.

After David left, due to dancing last night and the activities with David all night, my whole body felt sore, so I fell into a deep sleep again.

When I woke up and looked at the clock, it was already 12 o'clock. I was contemplating whether to get up or continue lying down when the phone rang. It turned out to be Leif calling.

"Hey, are you awake?" Leif asked.

"Not yet, just woke up. What's up?" I replied.

"I'll come to see you."

"Now?"

"Yeah, is it inconvenient?" he asked.

"No, I have nothing to do today, but it's almost time for lunch."

"Let's have lunch together."

"Okay." After all, I promised him today in the bathroom last night, and I didn't want to disappoint him. But mainly because I was exhausted from last night, if we did it again today, I would be completely worn out.

I got up and freshened up. Just past 12 o'clock, Leif called and suggested bringing some takeout for us to eat. I thought it was a good idea because I didn't feel like moving, so I asked him to bring the takeout.

In no time, Leif arrived. He looked even more handsome than yesterday, with his plaid shirt making him look more sunny and adorable. I thought he really resembled Oliver.

After having lunch, it was almost 1 o'clock, a perfect time to go to bed. We went to the bedroom together.

Leif couldn't wait and hugged me tightly, pressing his lips against mine, wild yet tender. I eagerly responded, savoring his passion. He slid his tongue into my mouth, and I responded with mine.

His hands began to wander all over my body. He roughly took off my shirt with one hand, caressing my skin, while the other hand unfastened my belt and stroked my lower body through my underwear.

Leif started kissing his way down my chin, neck, Adam's apple, collarbone, chest, and then began sucking on my nipples. He teased and sucked on them until they became erect, creating an intense sensation. I tilted my head back, panting heavily, emitting pleasurable moans from my throat.

He continued moving downward, kissing my abs, navel, until he reached my crotch that had already risen high in the center of my thighs.

With his tongue, Leif licked my cock through my underwear. He slowly pulled down my underwear with his teeth.

I looked down, his lips tracing the insides of my thighs, and my glans oozed clear juice.

I pulled him up, ripping off his outer clothes and pants. Through his white tight underwear, I could clearly see his cock trembling.

I knew he desired to be freed, so I pulled down his underwear. His already towering shaft fully presented itself before my eyes. Leif's cock was longer than David's, but not as thick.

I wanted to ask him why his cock was longer than David's, but chose to be a Bottom when he was with David, but then I thought that if I asked that, it would be betraying David.

Leif turned his head and we formed a 69 position, pleasuring each other orally. We sucked and licked each other's shafts passionately. My own cock was fully erect, with the purple head oozing juices that flowed down. He passionately licked and used his tongue to tease my scrotum, creating a warm and itchy sensation that brought immense pleasure and caused me to emit pleasurable moans.

With my moans, his actions became even gentler yet more intense. His tongue crawled along my shaft and onto my glans, rotating on the tip. The intense stimulation made my body tremble uncontrollably. He used his tongue to lick my frenulum, causing even more juices to flow out. Then he used both hands to hold onto my thighs and began sucking on my shaft.

He alternated between using his mouth to stroke up and down, using his mouth to shake his head while sucking on me, making my cock spin in his mouth. Sometimes he used his tongue to make circles around my glans. All the passion and tenderness concentrated in his mouth, transmitting endless pleasure to me.

With his movements, my body couldn't help but start to twist, actively thrusting my erect member into his mouth to match his rhythm. He seemed to enjoy this way as well, with more intense movements of his mouth.

At the same time, I also sucked on his hard and large cock, fully pleasuring him. I kissed every inch of his cock, alternating between tight, slow, fast, and gentle movements, using all my oral skills to tease his desire. Under my intense stimulation, his massive cock became even thicker and harder, showing his determination. He moaned continuously, while also sucking on my shaft.

At this moment, my hands were not idle. They wandered towards Leif's anal area, after lubricating with lubricant, I could feel him opening and closing, teasing and fingering him gently. His anus would truly convey his feelings. Leif's anus was very pleasing to the eye, especially smooth, and the color was quite tender. When I spread open the anus, I would find the tender inner walls even more tender.

Seeing this brought me immense pleasure. I pushed him away, making him kneel like a dog. After applying some lubricant to his anal area, I entered him from behind. Leif's anus wasn't tight, maybe because of David's thick member and frequent activities with him. My cock moved freely in Leif's tight hole, and it felt incredibly comfortable.

He quickly let out a pleasurable moan, especially loud, "Oh! Oh, yeah! Fuck me hard, pound me."

After thrusting from behind for a while, I turned him over.

To make it easier for penetration, I placed a pillow underneath him. I slightly pulled out the hard shaft that was fully buried inside him and gently pushed forward, gradually going deeper. I continued to slowly penetrate his anus, with each deep and shallow thrust, filling his anal cavity with my member. He seemed to enjoy the sensation of being completely filled. Seeing the opportune moment, I intensified my movements forcefully.

"Bro.! I love being fucked by you!" he said, acting spoiled.

Occasionally, I would use my glans to draw circles near his entrance, deliberately prolonging the time. I watched him twist his body, his face flushed, his mouth constantly uttering obscene words. I couldn't hold back anymore.

When he said "fuck me to death", without any warning, I forcefully plunged deep into his anus. He let out a loud "oh!" and I continued with vigorous piston-like movements. He cried out "oh! oh!" expressing the satisfaction that had been building up, fulfilling his desires. I allowed him to enjoy the pleasure of my dick rubbing against the walls of his anus, while he satisfied my desire for same-sex dominance. We both got what we wanted.

This boy in front of me, youthful and radiant, was exactly the type I liked. I really liked him! I would continue fucking him until he begged me. We fucked vigorously, drenched in sweat, our blood vessels pulsating, sharing each other's bodies. After a wild frenzy, we both reached climax simultaneously.

Finally, we came down from our orgasmic high and I asked him, "Between me and your boyfriend, who make you feel better?"

"Both of you make me feel great!" he replied.

Hearing that, I felt like maybe his boyfriend was still better.

As we chatted, he told me that he had been with David for over half a year, they often had sex, and they even had a threesome once. However, David didn't like seeing him being fucked by others, so they stopped doing that, although occasionally he would still go out to find someone.

"Would your boyfriend sleep with me?" I asked Leif.

"He's a top like you, how would you fuck together?" he said.

"Maybe your boyfriend can be versatile?" I playfully teased him.

"No way, he's amazing in bed. I've never heard of him bottoming," he replied.

"Oh," I finally responded.

In my heart, I thought that the sexual encounters between David, Leif, and me had become our secrets.

Chapter 5 Edward

Edward was not tall, probably around 170cm, and had a slim physique with fair skin. His dignified face carried a hint of childishness.

I met him online. At that time, I was spending Christmas at my boyfriend's house in City T (I'll write about that story later, for now, let's focus on Edward). After Christmas, my boyfriend went to work, and I was left alone in that big house, feeling bored during the day. Luckily, I had access to the internet and could chat online. That day, as soon as I opened Facebook, I noticed a message asking me to add him as a friend. He claimed to be Japanese and wanted to be friends. He even gave me a website link to his photos.

I thought, "This person is really boring. Why would an American pretend to be Japanese? Are foreigners highly sought after in the gay community in America?" As for the website link, I thought it might be a virus or something similar, so I didn't pay much attention to it.

After a while, he sent another message asking me to verify his request and kept emphasizing that he was really Japanese. Whether he was Japanese or American, it didn't matter to me for chatting, so I added him as a friend and started chatting.

He said he saw my information online and wanted to be friends with me. During our initial conversation, I really wasn't sure if he was Japanese, but rather thought he was an American with a fascination for foreign culture. His tone also seemed somewhat arrogant. So, I didn't have much enthusiasm to genuinely chat with him at the time, I just saw him as someone to pass the time with. Soon, those happy days came to an end, and I had to go back to school, bidding farewell to my boyfriend.

One evening, after returning to school, Edward started chatting with me online again. This time we had a long conversation, and I can't remember all the details, but the general idea was for me to believe him. He insisted that he was indeed Japanese and genuinely wanted to be friends with me. He kept emphasizing this, and at that moment, I started to believe he was Japanese. To confirm if he truly wanted to be friends with me, I said, "If you really want to be friends, then come to City H this weekend and we can meet."

Although he asked for my phone number, I still didn't take him seriously. But what happened next truly surprised me. On Saturday morning, while I was still asleep, I received a call from him, saying that he was on the train to City H and asked me to meet him at the station.

The feeling at that time was simply unbelievable. He took my joke seriously. I had no choice but to get up, get ready, and go to the station to meet him. When he arrived at the station, he called me, and I told him my location and described what I was wearing. To my surprise, he recognized me at first glance.

After meeting him, my first impression was that he was so thin and small compared to me, like completely different body types. At that moment, my heart seemed to have a slight impulse.

To prove that he was Japanese, he intentionally spoke some Japanese to me. I told him, "It doesn't matter if you are Japanese or not. Since you really came to City H, I'll consider you my friend." Actually, at that moment, I confirmed that he wasn't lying just from his unskilled English.

That day, I took him around City H. The city didn't really have much to offer, despite its reputation for delicious street food.

After spending the day with Edward, I booked him a room at the guesthouse on campus. I had planned to return to my dormitory after settling him in, but after getting the room, he persistently begged me to stay and keep him company. I told him I had a boyfriend, and we were just friends, so we couldn't do that kind of thing. At the time, my resolve was so firm, but in retrospect, how naive I was. Men are creatures who think with their lower parts.

What happened next went against my previous strong statement about having a boyfriend. After lying down, he climbed onto my bed and said he wanted to sleep while holding me, without doing anything else. When a cute and handsome boy embraces you, which gay wouldn't be moved?

His hands began to roam on my body, his lips on mine, wild yet tender. My defenses had already crumbled at that moment, and I wholeheartedly responded, savoring his passion. He extended his tongue into my mouth, and I responded with my own, intertwining and lingering, unable to stop. One hand caressed my chest muscles, while the other explored my lower region through my underwear.

I felt waves of passion coursing through my body as his hands ignited a fiery desire within me.

Edward climbed on top of me and started kissing my chin, neck, Adam's apple, collarbone, and chest muscles, then began sucking on my nipples. His actions made them hard. I felt so comfortable, tilting my head back, panting heavily, and letting out pleasurable moans from my throat.

Edward continued moving down, kissing my abs, navel, all the way until he reached the tent that had already risen in the center of my thighs. He used his tongue to tease my cock through my underwear, causing my body to tremble uncontrollably.

He quickly pulled my underwear down to my ankles, and with his head lowered, he lightly kissed my glans, then used his tongue to lick it up and down. I was gasping heavily, my excitement evident on my face. He took my shaft into his mouth in one gulp, and I felt an intense heat engulfing it. He started moving up and down, savoring my manhood, and it was clear that he was also enjoying himself.

My hands pressed against his head, following his movements, and I couldn't help but let out excited moans. He actively and rhythmically sucked, and I felt my cock growing harder and thicker in Edward's mouth.

He buried his head between my legs, greedily sniffing and kissing. His tongue traveled from the base to the tip of my erection, making my heart race. His tongue skillfully rotated and teased, rubbing against the corona, while his warm lips enveloped the protrusion, alternating between tightening and loosening, drawing it in and pushing it out. It was an indescribably wonderful sensation, and I quickly became uncontrollably hard. I watched his head bobbing up and down, and I was on the verge of climax.

I asked him to switch positions, and that's when I discovered how impressive his erection was, much larger than mine. I never expected that the petite Edward would possess such an enviable manhood. I used my hand to hold his erection, and my tongue playfully tickled his glans. Perhaps because it felt so pleasurable, he also let out moans. He was truly big, and I could barely fit his entire shaft in my mouth, while simultaneously stroking him up and down. He also sucked harder on my cock.

After a while, I couldn't resist the impending pleasure. I knew I was about to climax, to ejaculate.

I whispered his name, "Please, I'm going to come."

But he didn't stop; instead, he sucked even harder, and his tongue rubbed vigorously against the tie. I finally lost control, and my semen gushed out, straight into his mouth. I never expected him to swallow it all.

After I came, I energetically continued pleasuring his erection, but he didn't climax for a long time, and my cheeks were sore. It exhausted me. Afterward, he sat on my abdomen and began manually pleasuring himself, while I gently played with his nipples. Soon enough, he shouted and ejaculated a lot of semen, spraying it all over my chest.

That's how Edward and I had our first physical contact, our first experience of oral sex. After seeing him off on Sunday afternoon, I realized that I actually missed him. But I also felt guilty towards my boyfriend, and conflicting emotions occupied my heart.

I wanted to spend the following days peacefully, but being in a long-distance relationship with my boyfriend, I couldn't help feeling conflicted at times. I had the urge to cheat, but also felt guilty towards my boyfriend. I stopped contacting Edward, but found it hard to let go of my feelings for him, leaving myself unsure of what to do.

Life continued day by day, until one day Edward called and asked me to come to City A to see him. At first, I didn't want to go, but he persistently convinced me with his childishness, breaking down my defenses once again.

When I met him, it was already late evening. After he picked me up, he mentioned that he had plans to meet some friends for dinner. I was worried that it might be inconvenient for me to join, but he assured me that they were just ordinary friends. When we met them, I realized they were his colleagues - a man and a woman. Through their conversation during dinner, I could tell that Edward was doing well in his company and was liked by many. I thought maybe it was because of his outgoing personality and his ability to get along with people.

During the meal, he had a lot to drink, but seemed fine when we left the restaurant. However, once we got on the bus, he couldn't handle it anymore. He rested his head on my shoulder. At that moment, I felt touched and happy because I had someone who could lean on me quietly. The feeling is still vivid in my memory, as if I wished the bus would never reach its final stop, and we could just keep going.

When we reached his stop, I helped him off the bus. He was already feeling very heavy-headed, staggering as he walked. It was probably due to excessive drinking or an upset stomach. He immediately squatted by the roadside and started vomiting. Seeing him in discomfort, I felt a pang of heartache, and it felt like I was in love with him at that moment.

Finally, with great effort, I managed to bring him to his place. It was a well-decorated three-bedroom apartment, but with him living alone, it felt empty. I helped him into bed, undressed him, and he quickly fell asleep.

Sitting beside him, fully undressed, I watched him sleep, feeling indescribable emotions. As the night deepened, I held him close and peacefully drifted off to sleep.

The next morning, I woke up to the sound of his footsteps and found him drinking water. He asked me how we got back.

I said, "You gave me such a hard time last night. You're so skinny, yet so difficult. You should thank me."

"How should I thank you?" he asked.

"You figure it out," I replied.

"Alright then." He had a mischievous smile on his face as he climbed onto the bed, pulling down my blanket.

"You're already erect," he pointed at my cock.

Because I usually sleep naked, I was completely exposed in front of him.

"It's normal for men to have morning erections. You idiot," I replied.

Edward leaned down, using his tongue to lick and nibble on my ear. His wet and hot tongue twirled around, deeply penetrating inside and then engulfing my ear. The tingling sensation spread throughout my body.

Under Edward's skillful teasing, I felt a wave of heat rushing through me, and every cell in my body longed for his touch and teasing. I reciprocated his affection, wrapping my hands around his neck, eagerly seeking his kisses.

He trailed down my body, and soon his mouth grazed against my glans. He opened his lips and used the tip of his tongue to play with my glans, then pressed his tongue tightly against the sensitive frenulum beneath my glans, licking it from the bottom up towards the urethral opening. When his tongue reached the raised ridge above the glans, he retraced his steps and continued his licking. Under his intense stimulation, I couldn't help but moan in excitement.

Edward started to take my glans into his mouth, forcefully spreading his jaws and swallowing it. After he took my glans into his mouth, his lips wrapped around the prominent ridge behind the glans. His lips tightened slightly as he began to move up and down. The friction between his tongue and my glans felt incredibly pleasurable. I couldn't bear the immense pleasure and stimulation.

Suddenly, he spread saliva on my glans, then applied some on his anus. He straddled me, grasping my rounded glans and aimed it at his entrance. Maybe he was a bit nervous, as he tried a few times before successfully penetrating. I felt my hard cock deeply enter his entrance; his tender walls enveloped my cock. He slowly increased the frequency of his thrusts, repeatedly allowing me to penetrate deeply.

I looked up as I saw my cock moving in and out of his anus, feeling incredibly pleasurable! I followed what I had seen in gay films, slowly pulling out my cock, rubbing against the entrance of his anus, then suddenly thrusting back in, causing him to scream in pleasure. His reactions were intense; he writhed his body even more vigorously. I used both hands to firmly pinch his nipples, making them erect. It seemed like he was enjoying it a lot too.

I lost track of time as we heard the sound of our bodies colliding... We kept changing positions, doggy style, missionary, sideways. I was drenched in sweat from all the movements.

At this moment, we were both enjoying ourselves. I held onto my cock and thrust it all the way in, causing him to let out a scream. I watched as my cock moved in and out of this pink little hole, feeling an incredible pleasure. I was full of energy, feeling every thrust entering a mysterious territory in his body, and couldn't help but want to go deeper.

After a while, I pulled him to the edge of the bed, letting him lie down while I stood on the floor, spreading his legs apart and thrusting forcefully.

Time passed, and Edward began to use his hands to stroke his own cock. His movements became faster, and I was also reaching the peak of climax. At this moment, I increased the speed of my thrusts until finally, with a loud cry, my cock pulsated and hot semen shot into his entrance. Soon, his semen also ejaculated, and as I looked down, my semen flowed out from his anus, wetting a large area of the bedsheet.

That was how the sex ended.

Afterwards, we would occasionally meet and make love, but as time went by, the novelty between us diminished and gradually faded. I never knew what caused us to lose contact. Now, the only thing left is a photo he gave me.

Speaking of which, he was the first Japanese person I met. Later, I got to know a German gay through emails, as well as someone from England. They weren't the foreign people I had imagined. The only person I still miss now is Edward. Here, I can only remotely wish him health, safety, and happiness, just like the blessing he originally gave me.

Chapter 6 Clark

Speaking of Clark, one word can describe him: promiscuous.

When I first met him, I didn't have this feeling. It was a Saturday afternoon when we first met. I had just finished lunch and was bored, so I opened a chat room to see if there were any handsome guys to flirt with.

Soon, I started chatting with someone using the screen name "Dream Lover." He said he was 23 years old and taught at a middle school. Since I had nothing else to do, I thought, why not have some fun and hook up with him? So, I invited him to meet me near my place. Before I knew it, he arrived - not too slim, not too fat, and his looks were okay, but not overly attractive. He seemed like a decent guy, so I took him to my place.

Once we were at my place, he seemed a bit uncomfortable and was speaking hesitantly. I directly told him not to be so uptight, as we both knew our intentions were just for pleasure. I generally don't like people who are overly hesitant and shy. It's not fun to play with someone like that, let alone experience any pleasure.

After some conversation, he started to relax a bit more.

I told him, "Let's take a shower, I can't wait any longer."

He headed towards the bathroom, and I couldn't resist adding, "Make sure you clean your backside."

While he was showering, I prepared the condoms and lubricant, and I also played a gay porn movie in the big TV. By the time he came out, I was already naked, and on the TV, two handsome men were engaging in oral sex. I particularly enjoy movies from this company because their models are very attractive, regardless of whether they're tops or bottoms, and they have impressive sizes.

He saw that I was aroused and walked over, sitting on the sofa. He had lost his previous shyness and started stroking my cock with his hand. I glanced down at his own cock, very small and only about 10 centimeters when hard. No wonder he said he didn't top. It seems his equipment wasn't up to par, so he had no choice but to bottom. Looks like he was naturally meant to be a bottom.

My cock was getting harder under Clark's touch, and I used my hand to press down on his head, signaling him to give me oral sex. He was really understanding and quickly took my whole cock into his mouth. It was warm and wet.

He buried his head between my legs, greedily sniffing and kissing. His tongue licked from the base to the tip, causing my heart to pound. His tongue skillfully rotated and teased, rubbing against the coronal part. His warm lips wrapped around my bulge, tightening and loosening, engulfing and releasing. The sensation was indescribable, and I quickly became uncontrollably erect.

He was skilled at oral sex, driving my whole body crazy with desire. I had him climb onto the sofa and raise his butt, exposing his anus completely. After applying some lubricant to his anus, I gently inserted a finger into his rectum. It was tight and tender.

Soon he began to adjust to my finger, and I added lubricant to another finger. As the first finger withdrew and reinserted, the two fingers went inside him side by side. He moaned in satisfaction and his butt started to move in coordination with my finger, rocking up and down and sideways.

Seeing that he had no discomfort, I was thrilled to continue. I added a third finger to the mix. Sometimes all three fingers entered and retreated together, sometimes they moved in batches, or I spread them out to push and probe his package, or I flipped them up and down to intentionally stimulate his prostate.

At this point, he was so aroused that he couldn't even speak clearly. Before long, he became so eager, completely different from before. Watching his anus hungrily try to swallow my three fingers, I felt great satisfaction. His flower-like anus was still tender and delicate, thanks to the lubricant.

My three fingers continued to play with his tight hole, while I took out a condom and put it on my cock, also applying lubricant. Now everything was ready, just waiting to penetrate. As the three fingers were drawn out, without giving him any warning, I thrust my cock into his anus. Already accustomed to my three fingers, he immediately sensed the change and couldn't help but let out a cry.

I held onto his shoulders and waist, and my cock went full force, thrusting left and right, forward and backward inside him. Soon he started to move his butt up and down, sometimes fast, sometimes slow, tightening and releasing. His moans grew louder and louder.

The man as a top on TV was thrusting faster and faster, and I thought they might be reaching climax. Actually, I could also cum, but I didn't want to end the fight just yet. I wanted to fuck Clark so that he would never forget me.

I flipped him 180 degrees, making him lie on the sofa, and put his legs on my shoulders. With my hand supporting my cock, I thrust into his tight hole and continued pounding him. His moans grew louder and louder.

Finally, under his urging for me to cum quickly, I shot out my thick semen. After my orgasm, I pulled my hard rod out of his hole, and I could feel the warmth of my semen in the condom. I poured the semen out of the condom onto his cock. At this point, Clark started to jerk off with my cum as the lubricant. It didn't take long before he shot his own load, almost hitting my couch.

And so, the first time with Clark came to an end, and it was a perfect experience. He could be my sexual partner.

In the following days, he often called me and asked if I was free on weekends. Occasionally, I would still have sex with him. During that time, I also learned that he loved playing with multiple partners. I suggested trying it sometime, and he quickly agreed, even mentioning that we should find well-endowed men with big cocks for the experience.

Soon, this idea became a reality.

That afternoon, I called Grover and Albert. Grover was a versatile, while Albert was a top. I thought it would be exciting to have Grover with Clark as a bottom, and Albert with me as tops.

That evening, we all gathered at Grover's house. He had a big bed, nicely decorated. Four of us engaging in a group sexual encounter, it was quite lascivious.

Although Albert was the designated a top, I had previously played a 69 game with him. His oral skills were exceptional, and that experience left me trembling with pleasure. If I were to be the bottom, I would surely be fucked senseless by Albert.

We started with Albert giving me a blowjob because I enjoyed his mouthwork. My cock was enveloped by his warm and soft lips. With a slight push, I made my cock plunge into the depths of his mouth, instantly feeling the warm oral cavity stimulating my glans. It was so cozy, as he expertly wrapped his mouth around my cock, not too tight or loose, just the right amount of pressure. The friction between my cock and his mouth emitted a delightful smacking sound.

Meanwhile, Grover and Clark engaged in a passionate exchange. Clark greedily sucked Grover's cock while Grover played with Clark's asshole.

Suddenly, I noticed something in Grover's hand upon closer inspection—it was an anal plug. He alternated between licking Clark's asshole and teasing his little hole with the plug. It was the first time I saw someone using such a sexual device, and it vibrated. In no time, the plug was inserted into Clark's asshole, and as Grover turned on the switch, it began vibrating. Clark became exceptionally excited, moaning loudly. They were both quite excited.

Watching this debauched scene was truly captivating. Seeing Clark act so lewdly, I couldn't resist and wanted to thrust my cock deep into his asshole. However, Grover didn't allow it. He said he wanted to go first. Apparently, Grover didn't want to be the bottom and preferred to be the top this time.

Three tops fucking one bottom, it might be intimidating, but Clark didn't object to Grover's decision. After all, Clark was here at my request, and I didn't want him to be overwhelmed. So, I let Grover find another bottom to join us; otherwise, Clark might not be able to handle it.

Grover was not one to miss out on the action. He had already arranged for another bottom to join us (he referred to this internet friend as a bottom). When this person arrived, he revealed that he was versatile. I didn't know his exact name, so let's call him V.

While waiting for V to arrive, Grover had Clark lie on the bed. Grover raised Clark's legs and thrust into his tight asshole with force. Although Grover's cock wasn't big like Albert's, he was around 30 years old and had plenty of experience.

Sometimes, we could see Clark's flesh sinking deeply into his asshole, and when Grover pulled out, his rectum would protrude, looking delicate and enticing. As Grover fucked Clark, my cock was still in Albert's mouth, and occasionally, we would all pause and watch them make love.

Later, we took a break. Albert took Clark's cock into his mouth, and I sat on Clark's chest, sliding my cock into his mouth. Suddenly, the four of us became one entity. I fucked Clark's mouth with my cock, Grover pounded Clark's asshole, and Albert had Clark's cock in his mouth.

We maintained this position for a long time, and finally, Grover came, collapsing afterward. Seeing him climax, I withdrew my cock from Clark's mouth and put on a condom from the bed. Clark remained lying down. Thanks to Grover having fucked Clark previously, my cock effortlessly slid deep into his loosened asshole.

To be honest, it's difficult to describe the sensations we felt at that moment. It was incredibly arousing. As Clark was in a doggy style position, with Albert's cock in his mouth and my cock moving in and out of his asshole, V arrived. After a brief conversation between V and Grover in the living room, V entered the bedroom.

Seeing the three of us engaging in passionate sex on the bed, he said, "Wait for me."

V quickly undressed. His cock was large, even more attractive than Clark's. At that moment, I wanted to fuck V.

After joining us on the bed, V began to caress us. He used his hands to touch Clark's asshole, experiencing the sensation of me fucking Clark. Sometimes, he deliberately spread Clark's ass cheeks with his hands, making it easier for me to enter.

Noticing my well-built physique, V touched my chest muscles with his hands. I took the opportunity to press my lips against his, and he skillfully inserted his tongue into my mouth. With V, I alternated between passionate kissing and fucking Clark—it was truly amazing.

Whispering in V's ear, I said, "I want to fuck you. Is that okay?"

"Oh, come on," he responded.

Seeing his agreement, I had him lie down, and Albert, watching me pull my cock out of Clark's asshole, put on a condom and inserted his own cock into Clark's ass.

I raised V's legs high, exposing his round buttocks and pink asshole.

I had Grover, who was sitting by the bed watching, apply some lube to V's asshole. Grover lubricated V's asshole with his fingers, even inserting them a few times. After applying enough lube, I gently pressed my cock against V's asshole, grinding against it. Under my stimulation, V soon began to squirm.

"Faster, come inside," he pleaded.

I saw his desire, so I forcefully thrust, and my glans immediately submerged into V's tight asshole. His little hole was slightly tight, so I entered slowly. V's expression also showed a hint of grimace, probably because it was a bit painful.

I slowly and gently moved my cock, and V started to relax a bit, coordinating his breathing. He began to rhythmically contract his sphincter muscles, gradually accommodating my entire shaft into his asshole. Looking down, it was already fully engulfed.

Watching that tender and pink tight entrance rhythmically contract, squeezing my cock, I felt incredibly pleasurable, and my cock grew even harder. Sensing that V had adjusted, I started to thrust rapidly into his tight hole, feeling the friction of his soft and tender flesh walls against my glans and shaft. I looked down at V; he closed his eyes tightly, his eyebrows furrowed, and he began to emit faint moans. With each thrust, his moans grew louder, and his upper body kept writhing.

At this point, Grover climbed onto V's abdomen and started giving him a blowjob.

I looked over and saw that Albert and Clark were both extremely excited. Albert forcefully penetrated Clark's asshole, thrusting deep and hard. Each thrust seemed to pull the flesh walls from deep within. Every insertion was deep, every withdrawal was relentless. Clark tightly grasped the bedsheets, trying to raise his round ass to meet Albert's merciless thrusts.

Under the dual assault from me and Grover, V seemed particularly aroused. He used his hands to pinch my nipples, spurring me to thrust forcefully into his rectum. Every thrust almost pulled my entire length out before fully pushing back in. The intense physical stimulation made me feel insatiable.

I felt myself getting closer to the edge, my thrusts becoming narrower in amplitude but faster in speed, and I began to moan loudly.

"I'm about to cum, oh... oh, my God..." I cried out.

As soon as the words left my mouth, a stream of milky white semen erupted forcefully, shooting out with great force. Finally, at that moment, I released all the tension and my ejaculate sprayed wildly.

Exhausted, I lay on the bed, not wanting to move at all. Grover even helped me remove the condom filled with semen.

At this moment, I saw Clark's legs hooked around Albert's back. Albert seemed to have endless energy. His face was flushed, his muscular body swayed, his firm buttocks arched, the heat of sweat streamed down as he gasped heavily. He thrust forcefully and steadily, pounding Clark underneath him.

After I came, I felt like Clark and Albert's joyful and blissful moment had no end. It was as if time stopped. Albert's fervent caresses on Clark, with varying intensity, alternating between faster and slower rhythms. Clark clung onto Albert's back, wave after wave of excitement washing over him.

Albert's cock continued to thrust. After a while, Albert's body stiffened. He gasped heavily, his scrotum tightened, thighs clenched, and his entire body trembled as his cock contracted vigorously. It seemed that Albert had ejaculated, as he continued to spray out hot and thick streams of semen.

After pulling out his cock and the condom, Albert said, "I'm exhausted."

The three of us, I observed, saw Clark still lying down, breathing heavily, while Albert was sweating profusely.

The lovemaking between them thrilled the three of us. Why do people enjoy group sex? Is it because sex feels good? I don't think so. Perhaps the enjoyment of group sex lies in watching others being intimate. Watching from the sidelines is equally exciting.

At this moment, V sat up and pulled Clark's legs towards him. Clark hadn't understood what was going on yet, but V had already put on a condom.

"No, I can't handle it anymore. That three guys have already fucked me, I really can't take it," Clark exclaimed.

But V didn't care about Clark's feelings, "Didn't you enjoy it when I fucked you last time? Didn't you want me to fuck you again?"

It was only then that I realized that Clark and V had also been together. It turned out that this city was so small.

At this moment, I finally understood what kind of person Clark was. It seemed like he was becoming a public commodity.

"You little slut, I'm going to fuck you!" V teased.

"No..." Clark had no strength to respond anymore and continued to gasp heavily.

At this point, Clark's anal opening was already moist, and V didn't even need to apply any lubrication. He thrust his massive glans into Clark's asshole without any hesitation. With a squelching sound, V's cock went all the way into Clark's body.

"Oh," Clark moaned softly.

"Baby, I'm going to start moving," V said.

"Hmm," Clark nodded in agreement.

V indeed began to thrust his thick cock, but he deliberately inserted it slowly, then pulled it out, inserted it again, and repeated this motion over ten times. Sometimes, he would even completely withdraw his cock and rub it against Clark's tight asshole.

Clark started to scream, "Fuck me! Don't torture me!"

"Do you want me to fuck you?" V teased Clark purposely.

"Yes, fuck me hard," Clark replied.

V then rapidly thrust his thick cock, pulling out completely with each stroke, leaving only the glans inside Clark's anus, before forcefully thrusting it all the way in again. His lower abdomen vigorously collided with Clark's buttocks, filling the bedroom with the sound of their flesh pounding together. At the same time, V didn't neglect Clark's ears and used his nimble tongue to passionately caress Clark's earlobes. The intense stimulation on his ears and the unfamiliar pleasure from being penetrated caused Clark's body to contort unnaturally and his hips to twist lasciviously in response to V's thrusts.

"This feels fucking amazing!" V shouted at the three of us sitting on the edge of the bed, watching them make love.

Albert added, "Go all out, he's such a slut."

V's thick member was tightly enveloped by Clark's velvety rectal walls. Every thrust made him feel pleasure radiating from every cell of his cock, an indescribable satisfaction. V increased the frequency and strength of his thrusts.

"No, no, I can't take it anymore," Clark cried out in pain.

V ignored Clark's pleas, too consumed with his own pleasure. His speed became faster and faster, until his erect cock's flesh was rubbing hard against Clark's tightened rectum, finally reaching climax. He ejaculated in spurts, only stopping after releasing a large amount of semen.

Instead of allowing V to remove his member, Clark vigorously began to masturbate himself. In no time at all, Clark shot thick jets of semen into the air.

And so, a group sex session involving five people ended.

Clark was fucked by all four of us, and I also had sex with V.

It felt great, but for such activities, safety was paramount. To all those who yearn for and are addicted to group sex, I want to say: for everlasting happiness, all men need to have protection.

Chapter 7 Outdoor Sex

Speaking of outdoor sex, I think there are very few people in this circle who haven't tried it.

Looking back now, I find it quite exhilarating. Why did I choose to have outdoor sex? Well, it's because there was nowhere else to go, so we had to settle for playing in the great outdoors.

I've had many experiences of outdoor sex. The first time was when I had just entered this circle, and back then, I was still quite innocent.

It was the year I was about to graduate from my fourth year of college. I had been chatting online with a netizen for a long time. I still remember his online username: Mogul.

Finally, one day, he suggested that we meet up. At that time, I wasn't as crazy as I am now, so I thought, why not just meet up? Nothing bad would happen, right?

That night, at around 9 p.m., I met him at a bus stop near our school. He looked to be around 29, while I was 24 at the time. He was average-looking, not quite what I had expected, but decent enough.

After meeting, we strolled along the road, chatting.

At that moment, he said to me, "Do you want to find a place to have some fun?"

I was surprised by his words, but I was also somewhat curious. After all, I had just started exploring this kind of thing and was quite interested.

So, I agreed and asked him, "Where do you want to go?"

"Isn't there a secluded place nearby?"

"What? You mean outdoors?" I was shocked.

"Yes, I don't have a place either, so let's find somewhere without anyone."

Although I had reservations in my heart, I still agreed.

On the side of the road, there were some houses scheduled for demolition. The windows and everything were already gone. So, he and I sneaked inside. We found a wall facing away from the road, and he hugged me tightly. He seemed to be quite experienced. His hands slipped into my clothes and teased my nipples. It instantly made me feel very comfortable, tickling my nipples, which were already erect.

He unbuttoned my shirt and used his mouth to lick my nipples, driving me crazy. With my erect member pushing against my jeans, I felt incredibly uncomfortable! But he was considerate, and knowing that my member was poking him through my pants, he reached down and unbuttoned my jeans, opening the zipper. I happened to not be wearing any underwear that day, so my hard member sprang out.

He gently grasped my member with his hand, using his fingertip to tease the coronal ridge, making it itch and feel even harder. After fondling me for a while, he knelt down and began using his mouth to suck my member. It was so thrilling! His oral skills were really good, neither too tight nor too loose, just right. His mouth was so warm and wet, with his tender flesh rubbing tightly against my member, making me feel really good.

Moreover, there were passing vehicles on the road at that time, and occasionally pedestrians would walk by, which made me both worried and excited. Perhaps the pleasure came from the excitement of the unknown.

That time, it was really pleasurable and unforgettable. Each time I was about to ejaculate, I had to divert my attention and distract myself so that the urge to climax would weaken a bit, allowing me to prolong the experience.

After some time, I finally released my hot semen into his mouth. When I climaxed, my glans became incredibly sensitive, and I couldn't bear any more contact with it, but he still pecked at my glans with his mouth, which made me feel so ticklish.

I experienced the excitement of having sex in the wilderness and realized that having a partner with good oral skills makes it even more pleasurable.

The second time I had outdoor sex was truly considered "to have sex".

It happened when I was studying for my postgraduate degree. I was living in a dormitory and didn't have my own space to satisfy my desires. Although I could relieve myself with my right hand, using it every day started to feel dull. Masturbating had become a monotonous routine, with my mind fantasizing about the same scenes and my stroking speed feeling unchanged. Sometimes it would take longer to ejaculate, but the pleasure was always the same.

It was another night when I met a guy from our school online. He was from a nearby faculty apartment because it was close to our school. We chatted online, asking the usual questions like what roles we were playing, top or bottom, what we liked, and if we had a place to go. Because I am mundane and mediocre, I only asked those questions. But I felt like I was different from those people who intentionally tried to act cool, pretending to be chaste when they were actually promiscuous.

After asking him, I found out that he didn't have a place either. What should we do then? I was desperate because I couldn't control my desires when they arose.

Finally, he said, "How about doing it outdoors?"

Once again, the other person suggested this idea, and because I had one previous experience of outdoor sex, I agreed to it.

When I saw him, he was around 175 cm, but he had a delicate and charming appearance, giving off an attractive aura. However, he didn't have a fake or artificial vibe at all.

Surprisingly, he was quite daring. He led me to the corridor of a high-rise apartment in the faculty area. He explained that generally, people in high-rise apartments don't use the stairs, which was why he brought me here. It was probably already past 10 p.m., and there were few people going up and down the stairs.

We couldn't waste any more time since we were already here. We couldn't linger because this place wasn't very safe, especially since it was in our school's faculty residential area.

He quickly undid my pants, and just as time seemed to be running out, he wanted to give me oral sex.

I pulled him up and started kissing him. I rarely kiss others, only occasionally when I have a crush on someone.

Why did I kiss him? I wasn't sure myself, maybe because he had a delicate appearance and I kind of liked him. Additionally, I always had a strange thought in my mind that the more I liked someone, the less aggressive I would be in bed. It was probably because I couldn't bear to mistreat someone I liked.

While kissing him, my hand slipped into his underwear and felt his hard and erect cock. It was hard, big, thick, and felt great to touch.

I whispered in his ear, "With such a great tool, why do you still prefer being the passive one?"

"Yeah, I just prefer being the passive one. Being the active one is too tiring!"

Hearing this reason, I found it quite surprising, but upon further reflection, being the active one might indeed be exhausting, not just physically but also in terms of real-life responsibilities. Some passive partners demand their boyfriends to fulfill certain expectations and to behave in certain ways. This heavy reliance on the active partner might truly make them feel tired.

His hands were not idle either. He boldly exposed my cock and began to play with it. I pressed his head, signaling him to kneel down and give me oral sex. He obediently complied.

However, instead of directly taking my cock into his mouth, he teasingly used his tongue to flick my glans, which felt uncomfortable yet exhilarating, sending tingling sensations all over my body. I couldn't wait any longer. I forcefully pressed his head towards my genitalia, but he resisted my grip even more fiercely. He continued to tease my glans with his tongue in his own way.

He teased me gently for a while, driving my entire body into a frenzy. At this moment, he finally took my entire cock into his mouth. It felt so comfortable, wet, and warm in his mouth. He moved his hand up and down my shaft, and my hard cock sliding in and out of his mouth was incredibly satisfying.

Every now and then, he would stick out his tongue and tease my slightly open glans with it. After teasing my glans with his tongue for a while, he engulfed the entire head in his mouth. His tongue inside his mouth constantly flicked and teased the sensitive glans, making me unable to resist the ticklish stimulation.

I couldn't bear it anymore, and I pushed my hard rod forward, penetrating his wet and hot mouth. He started to vigorously bob his head, swallowing my rock-hard shaft.

After a while of teasing, I really wanted to penetrate him. So, I took out the condom I had brought from my pocket and handed it to him, indicating that he should put it on me.

Unexpectedly, he tore open the condom and brought it towards his own mouth, using his lips to hold the soft ring of the condom, just like a baby bottle nipple. With a slight suck, he gently sucked on the tip of the condom.

By this time, my erect giant shaft was protruding, and he quickly brought his mouth closer, enveloping the head of my cock with his lips. He forcefully pushed the condom using his lips, allowing my cock to gradually enter his mouth; when I felt the round glans touching the back of his throat, it felt so pleasurable and comfortable.

He licked my glans a few times with his mouth before standing up and supporting himself on the staircase railing. He arched his white buttocks, exposing his plump buttocks and tender anus.

Looking at his tightly closed anal opening, I gathered some saliva and applied it on my throbbing cock, stroking it back and forth to spread the saliva evenly. Then, I took some lubricants and applied them to his anus.

My finger rubbed against the anal opening a few times before I extended my index finger and inserted it into his body. I circled it a few times and rubbed it a few times. Stirring his anus, it started to itch, and he began to moan.

"Man, I'm going in!" I said to him.

I could tell he was excited, maybe just like me, because of the reason we were making love in this place. He seemed very thrilled. I twisted my body, and after rubbing my hard glans against his anus a few times, I plunged into his little rosebud, eliciting a sound of pain from him.

"Shh, keep it down!" I worried about getting caught.

Like this, with him arching his back, I fervently thrust in and out from behind, causing him to incessantly moan.

Being in this place, I couldn't be too reckless and couldn't use vulgar language. I could only silently ravish him, and in the quiet hallway, all I could hear were the sounds of our flesh colliding.

I lost track of time, and my hands tightly gripped his buttocks as my shaft repeatedly entered and exited his anus. Eventually, with increasing speed, I released stream after stream of my ejaculate.

I pulled my cock out of his anus, and he turned around and took off the condom from my cock.

Then I held him and teased his nipples with my hands, and soon he ejaculated white liquid all over with his hand. He sprayed it so far.

After we tidied up our clothes, we took the elevator downstairs, and that's how I concluded my second experience of having sex in the outdoors.

The third time I had sex outdoors was on a summer night.

The weather seemed gloomy. I had nothing to do, so I chatted online in the dormitory. At that time, I liked using Skype to chat and sometimes engage in passionate video calls with people. However, as time went by, I found video calls less exciting and lost their allure. They simply couldn't compare to the thrill of real encounters.

I remember on that night, somehow I connected with someone on Skype. During the video call, I noticed he was quite shy and seemed afraid that I might deceive him. But with my sweet words and relentless persuasion, he agreed to meet me. We had already agreed that if we felt compatible in person as we did in the video call, we would book a room. Unfortunately, the weather turned bad as it started to drizzle outside. Despite being caught in this dilemma, he still insisted on meeting.

Soon, he arrived at the designated place. It was dark since it was nighttime, and the streetlights weren't very bright. I vaguely recall him being tall, similar to me, with an average build. His face wasn't very clear, to be honest, I can't remember his appearance now. After exchanging a few greetings, I suggested going to a hotel room, but he insisted on returning home that night. I said it was alright since there were many cheap motels nearby. However, he advised against it, saying it would raise suspicions if we booked a room and didn't stay overnight.

Seeing his timid nature, I didn't expect that my daring proposal would make him enthusiastically agree.

I said, "How about doing it outdoors then?"

He readily agreed, but asked, "Outdoors? Where do you want to go?"

Nearby, there was a pedestrian bridge covered with billboards. In this small town, the pedestrian bridge was almost unused since people preferred crossing the road directly instead of bothering with the bridge. So, I suggested going to the pedestrian bridge since hardly anyone would be there.

It was already around 11 pm, and the streets were sparsely populated, except for the rushing cars on the road. We arrived at the pedestrian bridge, and he wasn't as shy as before. Instead, he confidently embraced me.

Due to the drizzling rain, I couldn't embrace him fully but had to hold an umbrella with one hand while hugging him with the other.

He wanted to kiss me, but I wasn't accustomed to kissing men, so we didn't lock lips but instead rubbed our faces against each other.

His hands were restless, wandering and probing in my crotch area. Honestly, I preferred my partner daring and audacious in bed. While we weren't in bed at that moment, I liked his initiative.

Soon, his hand had already slipped into my shorts. Since it was summer, I was wearing athletic shorts, which were particularly convenient, or, should I say, quite convenient.

His hands were skillful, stroking and manipulating my erect member. He passionately fondled and rubbed it. I could feel my shaft growing thicker and harder in his hand, igniting a wave of passion within me. I was getting impatient and overwhelmed with desire.

He understood exactly what a man needed in such a situation. He knelt down and enveloped my throbbing member with his wet lips.

I held the umbrella and watched him crouch down. I could only vaguely see his head moving back and forth. Though unable to see his expression clearly, I could truly feel his actions.

My member slid in and out of his mouth, his lips gliding up and down along its length. We were perfectly synchronized, thoroughly enjoying the intense pleasure. His oral skills made me feel incredibly comfortable, perhaps because it had been a long time since I last experienced this kind of passion, especially in such an exhilarating outdoor encounter.

He buried his head between my thighs, eagerly sniffing and kissing. His tongue traced from the base to the tip, making my heart race. His tongue cleverly rotated and teased, its tip caressing the glans. His warm lips enveloped my bulging member, alternately tightening and loosening, swallowing it in and out, creating indescribable sensations.

In his fervent sucking, I could feel my own climax approaching, the sensation of impending release, a surge of scorching heat about to burst forth. But at this moment, I didn't want to climax yet. I desired to make this outdoor encounter even more exhilarating.

So, I pulled him up and made him turn around, supporting himself on the bridge railing. He understood my intention, but he insisted on using a condom.

Fortunately, being someone experienced in such encounters, I had a condom in my pocket (someone may ask if I always carry condoms with me. Well, let me tell you: yes. Who knows when an unexpected encounter might happen).

I pulled down his pants to his knees, revealing his buttocks. He bent over, although I couldn't see his ass clearly in the dark,

I could feel that it was smooth and elastic to the touch. My right hand moved to his anus, which was clean and hairless. I applied some lubricant and gently inserted a finger, but he said it was uncomfortable and suggested using my cock directly.

I was initially worried that he might not be accustomed to it, but since he didn't need any finger preparation, it saved me the trouble. So, I quickly took out a condom from my pocket, put it on my erect member, and applied some lubricant. At this point, it was a bit challenging to hold an umbrella with one hand. He held onto the railing with one hand and spread his buttocks with the other, making it easier for my cock to enter.

With little effort, my glans had already penetrated his anus. I slowly thrust my shaft, feeling his synchronized breathing and his anus contracting and relaxing in response to my thrusts. Gradually, my entire member slid into his anus. When I looked down, it was completely engulfed.

Feeling his tight opening contracting rhythmically, it was incredibly pleasurable, and my cock grew even harder. After a while, it felt like he had adjusted, so I began thrusting into his tight hole quickly, savoring the sensation of his soft and tender walls rubbing against my glans and shaft.

The umbrella wasn't particularly large, and since he was bending over, raindrops hit him. But we were both too overwhelmed with passion, experiencing one climax after another.

I vigorously fucked him, sodomizing his tight asshole, creating slapping sounds. He moaned with each thrust, and I increased the speed, fucking him harder and deeper, hitting the deepest of his tight hole.

I lost track of time, but he seemed to be struggling a bit, asking me to cum faster.

Sometimes, I feel like I have a tendency towards sadomasochism. The more he begged for mercy, the more I wanted to fuck him hard.

After fucking him for a while in that position, seeing his discomfort, I increased the speed of my thrusts. The intensity escalated, and our bodies collided with louder impact, like a machine gradually gaining momentum and entering its highest speed.

"Oh... Oh..."

With my loud cry, I gave the final strong thrust, releasing my load explosively. After cumming, my cock gently rubbed against his anus, creating a delightful sensation.

Finally, with my hands stroking him, he came on the bridge. The outdoor encounter ended like that.

Later, I went through countless outdoor sexes. Looking back now, it truly felt exhilarating and satisfying. The only thing is, I can no longer remember their faces.

—-The End—-

Milton Keynes UK
Ingram Content Group UK Ltd.
UKHW022035301123
433552UK00015B/512